844 aa1

THE INTRUDER

DANIEL HURST

INKUBATOR
BOOKS

Published by Inkubator Books
www.inkubatorbooks.com

Copyright © 2022 by Daniel Hurst

ISBN (eBook): 978-1-83756-009-7
ISBN (Paperback): 978-1-83756-010-3
ISBN (Hardback): 978-1-83756-011-0

PROLOGUE

The sound of the woman screaming was muffled and barely audible above the rumble of the speeding engine. But the driver knew it was there because he had forced that woman into her current form of imprisonment only a few minutes ago before continuing his journey down these lonely country lanes.

Despite the drama he was orchestrating, the man behind the wheel was calm as he pressed his foot down on the accelerator and approached a bend in the road. But he didn't slow down for it, and his body leant into the curve as he rounded it before he straightened up again and increased his speed still further. While that corner had been comfortable for him, he wondered how it had been for the woman in the trunk. She would be rolling around and possibly bumping her head or at least her knees and elbows.

But that was none of his concern.

Nor was he concerned about the other passenger he had in this vehicle.

Glancing in his rear-view mirror, he saw the shape of the man on the back seat, his hands cuffed together in front of him and his eyes flitting from side to side, glancing out of the windows into the darkness and presumably wondering when this hellish evening was going to end. But it was far from over.

The driver had not yet got what he wanted.

Revenge.

He might have made a pretty good start of things by surprising his two passengers at their home and threatening them before bundling them into this car and setting off at speed. But there was still so much more he wanted. He wanted them to really suffer, just like he had, and he was sure that they would, unless they could somehow help him, a possibility that remained to be seen.

Another corner was taken a little too fast, and the driver heard a groan from the back seat as well as the muffled screams that continued from the trunk.

Perhaps he could put the radio on and drown out those other noises.

Or perhaps I'll leave it so I can carry on hearing them and taking pleasure from them.

There were no other vehicles out at this time, although that was hardly a surprise; it was the middle of the night, and everybody was surely in bed. The few homes that the solitary car passed certainly looked dark and quiet, and nobody inside them would have ever suspected that a crime was occurring right underneath their noses. This wasn't a part of the country known for its association with criminals, but there were plenty of laws being broken around here tonight, as there had been in the recent past.

Blackmail. Fraud. Trespassing. Assault with a deadly weapon. Speeding.

And there might be something else to add to that list soon.

Murder.

But that still hung in the balance. For now, the car powered on as the driver gripped the wheel tightly, and the handcuffed man wriggled in vain frustration.

And what of the woman in the trunk? Well, she kept screaming to be let out.

But would she get her wish and be set free?

And, more importantly, *Is that what she deserves?*

1

MARIA

Nobody likes waking up to the sound of screaming. It's disconcerting, not to mention alarming. But it's a sound I know well, and as I jump out of my bed and rush towards the distress piercing the early morning stillness, it's hard to believe that I was sleeping peacefully only a moment ago.

A quick glance at my bedside clock tells me it is not even 5 a.m. yet, although I could have guessed that from the lack of sunlight coming through the curtains. If all had gone well, then I would have slept for another hour at least before my alarm was due to stir me from my slumber and signal the start of a new day. But who needs an alarm clock when you have a six-year-old daughter who suffers with night terrors?

Reaching my daughter's bedroom while doing well not to bump into any walls or doorframes in my sleepy state, I rush towards my youngest in her bed, already uttering words designed to calm her down.

'Penny! It's okay. Mummy's here. Sshhh now,' I soothe. 'It's just a bad dream. Come on, what's the matter?'

I sit on the edge of her bed and grab one of her hands, not simply to comfort her but also to stop her from lashing out at me, as she has sometimes been known to do if she hasn't quite woken up from whatever nightmare is tormenting her. But she is awake, and as the screaming stops, a faint whimpering replaces it before she's trembling in my arms as I hold her vulnerable body and kiss the top of her soft hair.

'It's okay, darling. Everything's going to be okay,' I say, repeating a mantra I have said many times to her and my other child, Edward, who is three years older than his sister and has thankfully passed that stage where he wakes up in the night and needs one of his parents.

Edward is sleeping in his own bedroom, or at least I hope he is, although I wouldn't be surprised if all the noise coming from his little sister's room has woken him. But I'll go and check on him in a moment. For now, Penny is getting all my attention.

'Do you want to tell me what it was?' I ask, inviting her to share with me the cause of her distress. In the past, her nightmares have consisted of monsters under the bed, dragons at her window and some weird flying thing that she struggled to describe, but which she told me had got stuck in her hair, causing her to insist that she urgently needed a haircut as soon as she woke up. But it seems that today's bad dream will remain a mystery. Penny just shakes her head while remaining snuggled in my chest, so I let her know that she doesn't have to tell me if she doesn't want to before suggesting that she have a go at falling back to sleep.

'Will you stay with me?' Penny asks as she rests her head back on her pillow, and I tell her that I'll stay so she can close her eyes and feel safe again. I give it ten minutes before I hear her soft, breathy snores, and now I can relax because my little girl is at peace once again.

Until the next nightmare.

After leaving her bedroom, I poke my head into Edward's room and see my son curled up on his mattress with the duvet crumpled up on the floor beside his bed. He's always had a habit of getting too hot in the night and kicking it off, which is the exact opposite of how I sleep. I like to be wrapped up and warm if I'm to stand any chance of getting a good night's rest.

But a good night's rest is not what the gods have decreed for me on this particular occasion, because even though I get back into my own bed and attempt to snatch a few more minutes of sleep, it just isn't happening. Try as I might, I can never switch off my overactive brain once I've been woken up, so I already know that my aim of further sleep is a futile endeavour.

It's been that way for as long as I can remember. It takes me ages to fall asleep, and unless I get lucky and make it all the way to dawn without being disturbed, I won't get my eight hours. As a child, I would lie in my bed and stare up at the ceiling while imagining all sorts of wonderful things – like which toys I would play with the next day as well as reflecting on all the games I had played the day before. As I grew older, the thoughts that kept me up at night changed, but my brain's activity only increased with things like the dynamics of school and boys and friends and parties to worry about. Then I became an adult and discovered that work could dominate my thoughts: the deadlines, the office politics, the successes and failures and, most of all, the constant sense of unfulfilled ambition I felt as I wondered how I could best go about achieving my lofty goals.

For someone who struggles to relax, it perhaps wasn't the

wisest of moves to add two more sources of worry into my life in the form of my children, not that I regret their existence for one moment. But their presence means it has been a very long time since I got a good night's rest; I've spent several years now worrying about them both before and after they were born.

But at least there is one person in this house who has never struggled to sleep. That's the man lying next to me, the man who could sleep through an earthquake and actually did once while we were on holiday in California. It's William, my husband of twelve years, and a man whose snoring has sometimes threatened to be as loud as that earthquake that had me running to take futile cover under a kitchen table.

I glance across and smile as I see him how I often do, with his face mask on, his earplugs in and his mouth open slightly. It's no wonder he doesn't get woken up by noise or light considering his bedtime ensemble, but I don't begrudge his rest, as he's just as busy as I am once the alarm heralds the start of a new day.

But it hasn't sounded yet, and until it does, I need something to do, so that's why I reach out for my strategically placed laptop that's always there on my bedside table in case of times like this. It's far better to be productive now than to waste the next hour counting sheep, so I log on and start reading through a couple of emails that landed in my inbox overnight.

I might as well get a head start on the day.

I might as well tick off some easy tasks before all hell breaks loose around here in around fifty-eight minutes' time …

'MUM! THERE'S NO ORANGE JUICE!'

I roll my eyes at my son before asking if he has checked in

the utility room, where we usually keep the extra cartons. Of course, he hasn't, so he stomps off to check now, with his white school shirt hanging untucked over his black trousers and the tie around his neck still very much a 'work in progress'.

'Did you find some?' I ask when he returns, but he just grunts in reply before pouring himself a glass of juice while managing to spill a good portion of it on the kitchen table.

'Try to be more careful,' I tell him before wiping it up and checking in on Penny, who is currently chomping her way through a bowl of Coco Pops and making almost as much mess as her brother is.

This is breakfast time in the Gallagher household. It's crazy, it's chaotic, and it's routine. But it's also Friday, which means it's the last day of getting my two little ones ready for school before the respite of the weekend.

'William! Can you come and give me some help?' I call out as I struggle to make us our regular cups of coffee while ensuring our children aren't flicking milk at each other or spilling sticky juice all down their clean uniforms.

'Never fear, Daddy is here,' William announces as he breezes into the kitchen, his own uniform immaculate. He has always prided himself on his appearance and doesn't like to be seen looking anything other than his best. The bespoke suit he has picked out from his sizeable wardrobe today is one of the three he had tailor-made as a treat to himself for his fortieth birthday last year – and he looks a million dollars in it, which is apt because it cost a small fortune to have it cut to his exacting requirements. But that's my husband. He's a man who enjoys the finer things in life.

As well as his Gieves & Hawkes suits, he has a box of Honduran cigars in his study that only gets opened on special occasions, a couple of prestigious paintings that he insisted on being the top bidder for at a glitzy charity auction, which now hang in our dining room, and an Aston Martin DB11 on the driveway that's hardly practical for ferrying two little ones around, but he bought it anyway because he likes how it makes him feel when he's behind the wheel.

But, like his blissful sleep patterns, I don't begrudge him any of it because I know how hard he has worked to be able to afford those things. He might sleep like a baby and dress like a man who has never struggled a day in his life, I know the truth that William Gallagher has invested his own blood, sweat and tears into his work, and that is why he's in the position he's in today. It's why the school that our two children attend is an exclusive private one, and despite their current scruffy appearances, by the time I drop them at the school's imposing front gates, they will look just as smart as their father does.

'Here's your coffee,' I say as I hand William a cup before turning back to the gleaming Italian machine in the corner of our kitchen responsible for it.

'You're a star,' William tells me as he takes a small sip and reaches for a piece of toast from the plate in the centre of the table.

'Don't you forget it,' I tell him before I try some of my own coffee and feel that familiar buzz as the caffeine enters my system and lets me know that I'm going to be okay in making it through yet another sleep-deprived day.

'I take it that you didn't hear our daughter in the night?' I ask my husband as he ruffles Edward's dark hair before planting a good morning kiss on Penny's forehead.

'Huh?' he replies through a mouthful of toast, and I just laugh because that's obviously a no.

'She had another nightmare.'

'Oh no. Penelope, my dear girl. What was it? Tell Daddy everything!'

'Daddy, it's Penny!' she corrects him, her face scrunched

up in irritation, like it always does when her dad insists on calling her by her full name.

'Forgive me, Penny Penelope,' he singsongs teasingly as he tickles her, making her giggle so much I tell him to stop before she chokes on her cereal.

He continues to joke around with our kids while I complete a few of the more mundane tasks of parenthood like filling our children's lunchboxes and asking them where they left their rucksacks when they arrived home yesterday.

It's not that William is happy to see me do all the work around the home while he does the fun stuff. It's just that our expertise lies in different areas. I've always been more of an organiser, which is why I like to be the one in charge of things in the morning, whereas he plays the part of the 'morale booster', keeping spirits lifted so that our children don't get crabby and I don't get overwhelmed when the size and quantity of the day's tasks are threatening to overwhelm me. William takes on that role in many ways, from playing with our children and keeping them occupied so I can get things done without worrying about them, to making me laugh and calming me down whenever he can tell that I'm starting to get stressed. The two of us work well as a team, and that's good because it's not just in the home where we have to work together.

It's in the office too.

EDWARD AND PENNY were successfully dropped off at school on time, and thanks to the roads being quieter than they usually are at this time of the morning, William and I made it to our office well before our first meeting of the day. The six-storey commercial building towering over the smaller workplaces in this industrial park on the outskirts of town has been our business's home for the last five years. From the humble beginnings of working out of a tiny kitchen in a flat we shared in a down-at-heel part of London, we have grown our enterprise into the success story it is today, and I'm proud to say that Gallagher's Ad Agency has several hundred satisfied clients, all of whom contribute to average annual profits that run to well over a couple of million pounds. William and I are at the head of the good ship *Gallagher*, steering it through the choppy waters of the business world, navigating all sorts of obstacles on our path to where we believe the business really belongs, which is on the stock market.

But we're not there quite yet, which is why neither of us plans on slowing down anytime soon. In our roles as company directors, we oversee everything that happens in this office, from the targeting of new clients to making sure our existing customers are kept happy, as well as updating the shareholders and, indeed, the media on our progress. Business is booming, as evidenced by the lofty salaries we pay ourselves, but we aren't in danger of becoming complacent. We both have our eyes on the future, and who knows, one day it might be Edward and Penny taking over the reins. We started this company to create a better future for ourselves, but now we have children, the focus is on ensuring they have everything they ever need as they grow. That's why William and I are always first at the office and why one of us is usually the last to leave.

Our business is everything to us.

I like to think it is everything to our employees too, and just to make sure, I always go around the office and wish everybody a good morning before the more formal meetings commence. We're one big happy team here, and that's important because a unit is only as strong as its weakest link.

There are no weak links here.

This is a well-oiled, efficient machine.

Or at least I thought it was as I took my seat in Meeting

Room 1 on that sunny Friday morning and looked down from the sixth floor at the tidy pathways and ponds of the park opposite. Little did I know that somebody was standing in that park at that precise moment, looking up at this office and holding a very different opinion about what went on here.

An ex-employee.

An ex-employee we had been compelled to 'let go' six months ago.

An ex-employee who was difficult at the time.

An ex-employee who is still holding onto a grudge.

2

DAVID

I've been standing in the shade of this oak tree for over an hour already. Unbeknownst to the two owners of Gallagher's burgeoning ad agency, I got here way before their ridiculous car pulled up; a fact that would surely irritate them if they knew about it given the inordinate pride they take in always being the first ones through the door at work. But in reality I know that the couple wouldn't simply feel irritation if they knew I was here. They would feel surprise – and shock – quickly followed by a desire to call security and have me removed.

That's because, as I stand amongst the trees, out of view of any of the forty-one employees on the other side of the gleaming office windows, I'm acutely aware that I'm no longer welcome here. As has been the case ever since the day I was given an hour to clear my desk and hand in my security pass.

All thanks to an investigation into wrongdoing ... that found me guilty.

After which, the dynamic Gallagher duo had no choice but to 'regrettably' terminate my employment.

But there's just one problem with that.

I'm innocent.

And that fact has led me here today, to this part of town that was once a place I visited with pride. Landing a job as a junior account manager with an advertising agency like Gallagher's was a big deal for me. While it wasn't my first job, it had been my first one in this particular industry. After spending my twenties bouncing around in roles as varied as bartender, telemarketer and even a short, immeasurably dull stint as a lifeguard at a local pool, it might have seemed like I was suffering from a distinct lack of direction as my thirtieth birthday approached. I probably couldn't have argued against that assumption either. But then I saw the advert online seeking 'hungry and ambitious' candidates for a number of newly available 'creative sales' positions. Before I knew it, I'd hit the 'Apply' button and not thought too much about it until I was summoned to this office with several other candidates for an interview.

And it was there that I first met William and Maria Gallagher.

I'm guessing it was a surprise to all of the prospects in the interview process to come face to face with the owners of the company at that stage. We all presumed we would be interviewed by somebody a little less senior than the actual owners. But we were wrong. The husband-and-wife team explained that they took a keen personal interest in who was hired to their business, which was why they would be involved at every step of the way.

I felt nervous as I sat opposite the power couple, William in an expensive suit and Maria in a very smart ensemble, while I was merely sporting a cheap shirt I'd picked up at a discount store the day before. But the pair had put me at ease right away, chatting about my background and my hobbies before getting on to the main point of the conversation, which was whether or not I was the right man for the job.

That was where I'd expected to fall short. While I'd experienced a varied working life, I'd never worked at an ad agency before, so why would William and Maria overlook that shortfall to hire me? But I was wrong to lack confidence because the couple made it clear that they valued a candidate's potential far more than anything they might have done in their past.

The interview continued with a few 'role-play' exercises, ones in which I was required to demonstrate a creative side as well as a commercial one, mainly in coming up with innovative ideas for new campaigns while also managing existing customers. I let go of my anxieties and did the best I could before the interview concluded with a firm handshake from both William and Maria as they told me they would be in touch to let me know either way.

I thought that would be it.

As I left the Gallagher office that day, pulling off my pathetic tie and untucking my cheap shirt, I never expected to be in this part of town again.

That was until I received the phone call that told me I'd been the candidate who had most impressed.

After returning with a new suit and a spring in my step, I went about committing myself tirelessly to making my job a success. Having met William and Maria and learning that hard work, discipline and creativity were the backbone of their own achievements, I tried to model myself on them, arriving to work early, staying late and doing whatever I could to keep impressing those who had given me this chance. And my efforts had been well received for the most part.

Right up until the moment I was summoned into a meeting with the HR manager and informed that a complaint had been made against me.

I notice a steady stream of sharp-suited businesspeople coming and going from the glossy building opposite. But my own clothes feel tatty by comparison, and I'm gritting my teeth as I recall that fateful day when I first started here. I recognise a few of my former colleagues, and I can't help but feel a pang of jealousy at seeing their orderly, conventional lives while mine is in a state of disarray.

If anything, that's putting it mildly. My life isn't just in disarray, it's in a total and seemingly permanent decline, and it has been that way ever since I lost my job. With my only source of income gone, and stuck with a feeling far too bitter about what happened to me the last time I was an employee preventing me from even applying for a new job, there was only one thing in my life that made me feel like it was worth carrying on. That one thing was my fiancée, Debra, a woman I loved and a woman who loved me in equal measure, or at least until she learned of the reasons I was dismissed so unceremoniously from my job. Things had never been the same after that. The writing had been on the wall for a while, but it had still taken her a few months to pluck up the courage to leave me.

And now she has, I've lost everything.

My home, my dignity, the future we'd mapped out. Even my beloved dog.

Yet despite all that, life in and around this office seems to carry on as normal. Clients arrive for meetings. Delivery drivers drop off packages, and couriers bring important legal documents. And the couple who own this company sit up there in their lofty offices, safe in the knowledge that they will never struggle again in their lives. That last fact makes me one hundred percent sure that today will be the day I take action against them. Today will be the day I do what I have been thinking about doing for a long time.

Today will be the day I make that couple pay.

I am going to go into that office very soon and pay William and Maria a visit. But I can't just walk in and ask to see them. Not only would the receptionist prevent me from entering the upper floors, but that kind of arrival would also warn the couple of my presence, and I don't want them to know I'm coming for them. That's why I will take my time, stay calm and only strike when the moment is right.

Looking down at the rucksack by my feet, I think about all the things that are inside it. The wig. The dark glasses. The walking stick.

And the knife.

The first three items will help me get inside. The last item – well, that will help me get payback.

But it's still early. The working day hasn't long begun. That's why I pick up my rucksack and wander away, choosing to stroll around the park and mull over the details of my strategy some more. But I'll be back very soon. Lunchtime probably.

I need a few more hours to ready myself.

After all, it isn't every day I execute a plan to kill somebody.

3

MARIA

I 've been so busy this week that I completely forgot that William and I were due to attend an awards ceremony today. Last month, by way of an embossed letter, we found out that we'd been nominated for 'Best Business' by our town's mayor. I was thrilled when I read the news.

It really was an honour for us to be recognised in our local area, although William was slightly less excited about it. We've been nominated twice before and failed to win, so he was hardly enthusiastic about the prospect of making it a hat-trick of failures. Nevertheless, I contacted the mayor's office and let them know we would be in attendance when the winner was announced, which is why it would have been extremely embarrassing if I'd actually forgotten to go. But thanks to a synched diary reminder on my phone, disaster was averted, and William and I are now on our way, having left the office just before lunchtime in order to make it for the start of the ceremony at midday. Fortunately, we were dressed smartly enough today not to have to go home and change, so that's saved us some time, and while I had taken a salad into the office for my lunch, it's hardly the end of the world that I won't get to eat it now.

Like most of these occasions, the awards are only a small part of the event. The main part consists of a luncheon and drinks where the two hundred or so attendees will get to chat to each other over a light meal and perhaps a glass or two of champagne. The mayor will be on the top table, looking down over the residents of his town and quaffing his drink of choice, while the rest of us will sit nervously waiting to find out if we will get to join him onstage to receive our honours.

William and I usually work through our lunch hours, a habit we have held ever since we went into business. Back then our work ethic was driven by how paranoid we were about our fledgling business failing, but these days we work so much simply because there is so much work to do. But we're allowing ourselves this rare break today in order to show our faces here, although William is still mumbling about this potentially being a massive waste of time – and source of considerable awkwardness – if we come up short again.

I gently remind him it's the taking part that counts before suggesting it's good for us to network with other local busi-ness owners – there is no telling what opportunities that might lead to in the future. I must do a good job of persuading him that being here isn't such a bad idea because he stops complaining as soon as we walk into the hotel hosting the awards ceremony, or perhaps his smile is more down to the fact that he has just been handed a very tall glass of champagne. I guess I'll be the one driving us back to the office.

I'm feeling optimistic as I enter the function room and gaze across the sea of tables, one of which will be where we are to sit for the next couple of hours. It's not the easiest job in the world to find out which place settings have our names on them, but we eventually manage it, and by the time we've taken our seats and introduced ourselves to the other people on our table, I'm feeling more relaxed than I can ever remember feeling at this time in the working day.

All heads turn when a man wearing the robes and gold chain of office around his neck enters the room and gives us all a rather royal wave. The mayor is here, resplendent in the civic regalia of his official position.

'Do you think it's real gold?' a young woman at our table whispers as we all swivel to admire the mayor's heavy chain as he takes his seat and the event commences.

I enjoy a lovely lunch of salmon fillet, lightly steamed vegetables and a crunchy bread roll, while William has a Spanish chicken stew washed down with enough wine to make it clear that I really will have to do the rest of the driving – not to mention work – this afternoon. Then, once all the plates have been cleared away, the glasses topped up again, and a selection of minor awards have been met with gracious applause, it's time.

It's time to find out who has won the main award.

A hush falls across the room as the mayor once more picks up the microphone and makes a couple of pretty bad jokes that we all laugh at just to be polite. Then, with a flourish, he opens the envelope handed to him, and I reach out to squeeze William's fingers beneath the table.

'And the winner of the Best Business Award 2022 is ... Gallagher's Ad Agency!'

I don't believe it. We've only gone and won!

William looks almost as shocked as I am, but there's no doubt he's thanking his lucky stars that I persuaded him to come here today. He hugs me tight, and we get up from our seats to make our way through the packed room in the direction of the man holding our engraved glass award. I feel myself blushing with so many pairs of eyes on me, but William confidently strides up on to the stage with his hand outstretched, ready to greet the mayor and accept the award.

We both thank the mayor before turning to face the sizeable audience, and that's when I glance at my husband to let him know I'd prefer it if he would do the talking here.

Receiving the microphone, William clears his throat before embarking on his acceptance speech as I stand beside him, trying not to make eye contact with too many people because it will only make me blush even more.

'Wow, this is a nice surprise,' William says, looking down at the chunky flame-shaped trophy in his hands. 'I guess we've got ourselves a brand-new ornament for the Gallagher offices. What do you reckon, Mrs G?'

He proffers me the award, and more at ease now, I laugh, as does the audience. William has always had that easy-going way with people; he makes them relax. I wish I were as calm and cool as him in moments of pressure, but I do my best work out of the spotlight. My husband, though, is very much a man who shines brightest when under it.

'This is an incredible honour,' he continues, his tone more serious now. 'When Maria and I started our business, we had no idea if it would even be something the two of us could make a living from, so to stand here today as the recipient of the Best Business Award is truly remarkable. Thank you so much for those who voted for us and commiserations those of you who were also nominated, but I have to say, you would have all been worthy winners. It's truly a privilege for us to have been mentioned in the same breath as you all.'

That's my man. Being humble and acknowledging others.

In his twenties he might have been a little cocky, but now he's in his forties, he is mature enough to accept such an award with grace and self-deprecating humour.

'You know, it was my wife who convinced me we should be here today,' William admits. 'We very rarely leave the office during the day, and if it had been left to me, then we would probably have missed this, which would have proved to be a big regret – and a big mistake. But here we are, so how about a few words from my beautiful, amazing wife and business partner, Maria!'

I feel my breath catching in my throat as I realise William is handing the microphone over to me, and as I take it, I have absolutely no idea what I am going to say.

I wait for the applause to die down, which buys me a few precious seconds, but then the room is quiet again, and everyone is waiting for me to speak.

'Erm ... thank you,' I begin, nervous and unsure. 'Like my husband just said, it really is an honour for us to win this award.' I pause, aware there's something missing. 'But it's not just us, of course. We can't thank our brilliant team enough.' For a moment, I glance out at the room. 'And, like William also said, we now have a treasured ornament for our offices – or maybe we'll just put it in our dining room at home.'

I'm relieved when I get a laugh. I essentially stole William's joke, but I don't care because it seems to have worked. Now I just need to quit while I'm ahead, so I wrap it up. 'Thank you again for such an honour. Now, where's that champagne tray?'

I hold up the award as the audience smiles and raises their glasses. Cameras flash; then we make our way off the stage to more applause.

We finally get back to our seats, and I feel the tension leaving my body as I examine the newest member of our table, the trophy that confirms we really are the current holders of this town's Best Business Award.

We all make our way into the bar area, and as William and I mingle with other attendees, I'm really enjoying myself. I revel in the glow of victory, forgetting all about work deadlines and how busy I am as a mother.

The two of us get talking to a couple who run their own florist shop on the high street, and I let them know that not only have we heard of their business, but we've also used it several times, most recently ordering a beautiful bouquet for a friend who had lost her partner. We then get chatting about all sorts of things before the subject of television comes up, and William mentions that we are avid fans of true crime documentaries. The couple excitedly share that they love that genre too, before confessing that they often compete with each other to come up with the perfect way of committing a murder – and getting away with it.

I laugh at that until William admits he's already planned the perfect murder, or at least my murder anyway.

'Maria here is deathly allergic to peanuts, so I wouldn't have any trouble sprinkling a few of them into one of her meals and, hey presto, she's gone, and I can simply wipe away my tears and inform the police it was a mistake on the part of the local takeaway.'

The couple laugh, confident that William is just joking, and I laugh too although not before giving him a friendly slap on the arm to remind him that killing me is definitely off the menu. Then the conversation moves on to more mundane topics like how we each target new customers for our respective businesses, and while it's all still interesting, the crowd is starting to thin out, and it's not long before I suggest to William that we think about heading back to the office.

William seems like he would rather stay and keep exploiting the free bar, but I convince him to say his good-byes, and we leave the hotel, the award in our possession and a big grin on our faces as we make our way to our car beneath the bright sunlight of a lovely Friday afternoon.

4

DAVID

This is it. It's time. I'm going to do it. I'm going to go into that office and confront William and Maria. I am finally going to make them suffer like they made me suffer. It will be nothing more than they are owed.

My disguise is on, and I know I will be able to get past reception and make my way up to my former bosses' offices.

And that's where I will give them their big surprise.

I am experiencing a potent mixture of excitement and dread as I step out of the trees and make my way inside the boundaries of the industrial park. This is such a plain, uninteresting place. Nothing truly newsworthy ever happens here. Sure, some business deals get conducted along with plenty of backslapping and handshakes to signal a job well done, but nothing that would be deemed important enough to grace the front pages of the town's newspaper, let alone the national papers. But all that is about to change.

By the time I'm done, what has happened here will be making headlines around the country and, who knows, maybe even the world.

The thought that my name could be on people's lips in foreign lands seems very bizarre to me as I keep moving, slowly and deliberately, playing the part that my disguise demands, even if I'm not actually in sight of anybody just yet. I've never been one to court attention, but I'll be getting a lot of it soon. Okay, so most of the attention will be coming from the police, but there will still be plenty from others. Old friends. Old partners. Old classmates. They will all hear about what happened at this industrial park and shake their heads before most likely going on to say something along the lines of how they couldn't believe the person they had once known was capable of such a thing. And they would be right. The person they had once known could never have done what I am about to do now. But that person is long gone, and in his place is a heartless shell, devoid of anything but a single desire to right a wrong.

As I get closer to the office, I think of something that almost makes me stop and turn around. It would take a lot at this point for me to consider changing my mind, but that's exactly what it is. It's the thought of my parents and how they will react to the news that their son has turned into a murderous villain.

Will they still be capable of loving me after today? Probably not, but then again, maybe it's true what they say: that a parent will always love their child no matter what despicable acts they are responsible for. All I know is that I am certainly about to put that to the test.

But I won't stop. My mum and dad will be free to process their pain, anger and guilt however they see fit. Just like I am free to process mine in my own way.

And my way involves death.
Specifically, *the deaths of William and Maria.*

5

MARIA

I wave to a few of the people from the awards ceremony as I drive out of the car park while William sits beside me. He's examining the trophy and still grinning from ear to ear about it.

'Anyone would think you've won an Oscar,' I say to him, chuckling at how pleased he is with it. 'It's only a chunk of engraved glass.'

'But it's what it represents,' William tells me with a hiccup, which is what guzzling fizzy bubbles all afternoon will do, I suppose. 'It represents how far we've come. It represents us following our dreams. And it represents possibility. Of what might be next. Of what the future holds. Don't you think?'

'I think you've had too much to drink and shouldn't go back to the office,' I reply officiously, but I'm only joking and fully intend to drive the pair of us back there right now. But William latches onto my words and has another idea.

'Why don't we take the rest of the afternoon off?'

'What? We can't do that.'

'If we can't do it, then who can?'

'But we have work to do.'

'Let other people deal with it for once. And besides, it's Friday afternoon. The sun's shining. Nothing much happens now anyway. You know as well as I do that everyone in the office will be winding down for the weekend.'

'Yeah. That's precisely why we need to go back. To make sure they're still working.'

'We can trust them. We wouldn't have hired them if we couldn't.'

I raise my eyebrows at my husband because he should know that a group of employees are never going to work quite as hard with their boss out of the office as they would if their boss was present. It might have been a while since either of us were lower down the workplace ladder, but we can both still remember what it was like when somebody else was in charge of us. It's only human nature that people take it easier when they know they aren't being watched – on a Friday afternoon of all times.

'Let's just go back for an hour or so,' I suggest. 'Make sure everything is okay. We can still finish early. Just not this early.'

'You're missing the point,' William tells me, still turning the award over in his hands. 'We haven't worked so hard for all these years just to have a successful company or to make lots of money or to win fancy awards. We've worked hard so that we have freedom. But what's the point of having it if we never use it?'

I mull it over as I keep on driving us back towards our office, but I can see my husband's point. We should be able to make spontaneous decisions like whether or not to go home early and not feel guilty about them. So why don't we? It definitely isn't freedom if I can't relax when I'm not at the office.

'Maybe you're right,' I concede. 'But shouldn't we let the team know about the award?'

'I'm definitely right. It might be for the first time in my life, I'll give you that. But I am right on this occasion.'

We both laugh as I bring us to a stop at a red light, and now I have two options. I can go straight on, a route that will take us back to work. Or I can turn left, a route that will take us home.

'Okay, let's finish early. But let me quickly go and pick up some papers from my desk so I have them for the weekend.'

I feel like I'm offering a good compromise, and I'm all set to drive forward when these traffic lights turn green, but William isn't having any of it.

'I am not letting you take work home for the weekend. As the co-boss, I'm ordering you to have two full days of rest and relaxation, where the only work you are permitted to do is ask me to go to the fridge and get you another snack.'

I giggle at my husband and his light-hearted authoritative boss act. It's sweet of him that he wants me to relax now. But I know it's also because he's had a few drinks, and life always seems simpler when buoyed up by champagne, doesn't it? In reality, work still needs to get done whether he likes it or not, and I have a feeling he will realise that when he wakes up tomorrow and the fizz has worn off.

Then he'll probably be the one insisting we drive to the office on a Saturday.

'And as your co-boss, I am ordering you to listen to your wife and let her do what she thinks is best,' I instruct. 'I'll be two minutes. I'll grab the papers, let everyone know we've won, and then we'll go home.'

The light must be about to change. It feels like it's taking ages. Come on, go green. But it still hasn't, and that gives William a few more seconds to change my mind.

'If you go to the office, then I won't tell you what I was planning for this evening,' he says.

'What?'

'There's something fun we could do tonight. But I won't tell you what it is unless you take us home right this minute.'

'Don't be silly.'

'I'm not. If you drive straight on after these lights, then you'll never know all the wonderful things I was hoping we could do this evening.'

'If this involves me and you doing something *wonderful* in the bedroom, then I'd rather not hear it.'

'Hey!' William acts hurt, but I couldn't resist a cheeky swipe at him.

'What is it? I demand as the car next to me revs its engine, its driver even more impatient than I am to move again.

'I was thinking we could get a babysitter for the kids and go to Luciano's,' William says. 'A nice table for two. A bottle of wine. Your favourite pasta dish. An irresistible dessert. What do you say?'

I have to give it to my husband. That does sound good. An invite to our favourite Italian restaurant to overindulge in some delicious, creamy treats is definitely not easy to turn down. But, as usual, the practical part of my brain takes over then.

'It's a bit short notice to find a babysitter now,' I say. 'I doubt Cassie is free.'

'Then we'll find somebody else,' William replies, clearly entirely unconcerned.

'I'm not leaving the kids with somebody we don't know.'

'Then how about we ask your parents? They'd love to see their grandchildren.'

'But they might have plans of their own.'

'Your parents? I seriously doubt it. Your mum will probably be watching old episodes of some BBC comedy from the seventies while your dad snoozes in his armchair.'

'You make them sound so old!'

'Well, they are pretty old!'

'No, they're not! For all we know, they might have all sorts of exciting plans this evening.'

'Like what?'

'I don't know. They could be going out dancing or to watch a movie or for a romantic meal of their own.'

'Your dad can't dance, what with his hips, your mum wouldn't be able to hear the movie properly, and they never go for meals out anymore because they both have an endless list of food intolerances after a lifetime of eating the same thing for dinner every night. Am I right?'

My husband might be being a little cheeky about his in-laws, but I have to admit he's probably right. My parents are ageing, and they are definitely set in their ways. It's a pretty safe bet to presume they won't be going out this evening. But he is right about one thing. They would love to see their grandchildren. So maybe it's not the worst idea in the world.

'Okay, I've got another compromise,' I say, ever the negotiator. 'I'll ask my parents to have the kids, and if they say yes _'

'– which they will.'

'If they say yes, then we will drop them off at their house. It's less hassle for my parents if they can be in their own home. And then, rather than us two going out, we could have a meal at home. We never do that, do we?'

'The house to ourselves?'

'Exactly.'

I wink at William, and he is on my wavelength, so he doesn't try to talk me out of it. But he does remind me one more time that work really can wait until Monday, so as the lights finally change and the car beside me speeds away, I have decided what to do.

I won't be going straight on to the office. Instead, I indicate left and steer us towards home.

It seems like quite an inconsequential decision in the grand scheme of things.

But I might have just saved both of our lives.

Or at least delayed the inevitable ...

6

DAVID

I'm pretending to be blind as I walk through the automatic glass doors and enter Gallagher's Ad Agency. For full effect, I'm wearing a wig and dark sunglasses while holding a white stick out in front of my body. Once there, I pause, hoping that whoever is behind the reception desk will see that I might be unsure about where to go next, and come out from behind that desk to offer me some assistance.

I might be giving the impression I can't see anything, but of course I can see whatever I want to, and as I look over, I'm pleased the woman behind the desk isn't someone I recognise from my time working here. That makes things much easier. I spent my trips in and out of this office flirting with the previous receptionist – Kathy – so she'd have seen straight past my disguise. But this new young woman will never suspect that the blind man in front of her once worked here.

'Hi? Can I help you?'

She has made her way over to me and has a look of concern on her face, although it's one that she surely presumes I won't be able to pick up on.

'Oh, hello. Yes, I was hoping that you could. Am I in the Gallagher's Ad Agency offices?'

'Yes, that's right.'

'Oh, wonderful. I hoped my driver had taken me to the right place, but I can never be too sure, you see. My eyes aren't my biggest ally these days.'

A sympathetic expression is on the receptionist's face now, which is exactly what I'd been hoping for.

'Well, I can assure you that you are in the right place, sir. Do you have an appointment?'

'No, not quite. I'm here to visit a couple of old friends, but I was hoping to surprise them if possible. They don't know I'm coming.'

'Oh, okay. And who would they be?'

'William and Maria Gallagher.'

The receptionist looks surprised then, but I keep my cool.

'They're very old friends of mine. We used to work together, long before they made it big. We haven't seen each other for years. But I was hoping to catch them today while I'm in town on business. Would that be possible?'

'Oh, well. I'm not sure.'

The receptionist isn't quite saying what I want to hear, so I decide to play the sympathy card a little stronger.

'Things have been difficult for me since the loss of my eyesight,' I say, gesturing to the dark sunglasses that cover a pair of eyes that work just fine. 'I withdrew from society a little bit, if I'm honest, and in doing so, I lost touch with a lot of people. But I'm trying to put that right now, and I was hoping that today I would get the chance to see William and Maria, if only for a few moments. After all, I am sure they are very busy people.'

'Erm ...'

'I'm not often in town – it has been quite the journey today, and I'm not sure when I'll have this chance again –'

I'm really laying it on the receptionist now, pulling at her heartstrings, saying whatever I can to get her to let me go upstairs to see my old friends. But then she says something I hadn't planned for.

'I'm really sorry, but Mr and Mrs Gallagher aren't in the office right now.'

'They aren't?'

I can't believe it. All the time I worked here I never knew either William or Maria to leave the office outside normal working hours. Yet now, on the day I have come to 'catch up' with them, they are absent.

'Where are they?'

'I believe they're attending an awards ceremony in town.' She smiles. 'They've been nominated for Best Business 2022.'

I clench my fists at the thought of the couple who have wronged me being wined and dined at a fancy ceremony while I'm standing here with nothing to show for my life but the ridiculous disguise I am wearing. I'm so suddenly angry that I almost forget to stay in character and don't say anything for a moment. But, fortunately, the receptionist mistakes my silence for disappointment and has some better news for me.

'But they said they were going to come back to the office afterwards, so they should be back soon.'

I see her glance at the oversized clock on the wall, and things feel a lot more promising than they had a few moments ago.

'Oh, that's good. I'll wait for them, then. Could I perhaps sit in their office until they get back?'

The receptionist seems unsure about that request, and I expect she will just suggest I wait down here in reception instead. But I would much prefer if I could have the element of surprise upstairs in a quiet room rather than in this public space.

'I think it would really be a lovely surprise for them if I were waiting for them in their office. I won't get in the way, of course. I'll be very quiet.'

I smile at the receptionist then, hoping that will seal the deal. And it seems to do the trick because I see her glance across at a colleague entering the office behind me, and she asks that person if they wouldn't mind escorting me up to the sixth floor.

'Erm, yeah, sure,' he replies, barely looking up from his mobile phone, which is good news for me because I recognise him as someone I worked with when I was employed here. But the man doesn't pay any real attention to me, and as we make our way over to the lifts, it seems my plan is still very much on track.

I wait patiently while the lift descends, and when the doors open, I am invited to enter first.

'Just a couple of steps. That's it, you've got it. You're in,' my old colleague says, clearly trying his best to be of help to the person he's escorting.

'Thank you,' I reply before the doors close, and we begin our ascent.

I've stood in this lift many times before, but this time feels different. This time, I feel alive. That's because I'm not on my way to my desk or some boring meeting like I used to be.

I'm on my way to do something life changing.

The lift reaches the sixth floor, and I'm once again verbally directed before I am taken to William and Maria's office. I know the way, obviously, but I make sure to act as if I am having some difficulty being led so that the other workers on this floor won't suspect who I really am.

And then we arrive.

We are at the office belonging to the two people who so wronged me.

As I know from the past, this is a very impressive space, one that truly befits business owners like William and Maria. Two sleek, modern desks sit in front of a huge window that overlooks the park I have spent all morning lurking in. Expensively tended plants burst from tall pots in the corners, and a vast storage unit is adorned with framed certificates and awards, as well as photos of the couple who own this company, both of them tanned, fit and healthy on their numerous exotic holidays, either just the two of them or with their children. And there are plenty of files on the desks, showing how busy this pair is, as well as state-of-the-art computer screens to indicate how much cash the company likes to spend on its infrastructure.

There is no doubt that this is a stunning office, and the only problem with it right now is that its usual occupants are not here.

'Sorry, do you know exactly when William and Maria will be back from the awards ceremony?' I ask my former colleague, who is still standing awkwardly beside me.

'I'm afraid not. But can I get you anything while you wait? A coffee or a tea, perhaps?'

'No, I'm fine, thank you. I'll just wait for them.'

'Okay, well, you can have a seat just here,' he says, guiding me into a chair. 'And hopefully you won't have to wait too long.'

He leaves then, and I'm now on my own, sitting in the spacious office and staring at the photos on the shelves. The knife I carry is still hidden on my person, but it won't take me more than a second to pull it out when the couple walk in. But until then, I have little to do.

The clock on the wall keeps on ticking round and round, and the longer it goes on, the more it seems to taunt me. I am still no closer to confronting William and Maria. After thirty minutes pass, I begin to worry that the couple aren't going to come back at all, and as it reaches one hour, I realise they almost certainly aren't.

I can't believe it. What are the odds of them breaking their usual routine like this? It's as if they have been blessed by fate, forever destined to never be in the wrong place at the wrong time, immune to anything negative that might harm them. That is the exact opposite to my own experience of life. I have nothing but bad luck wherever I go, and today only seems to prove that point further.

William and Maria still haven't appeared, but some of their workers are clearly starting to take advantage of their bosses' absence as I look through the glass that separates this office from theirs to see people logging off from their work-stations a little earlier than usual and heading home for the weekend once they are confident that they won't be getting in trouble for it. That's when the door to the office opens again, and the ex-colleague who showed me up here apologises profusely for the delay before saying he's sorry, but he has just got word that William and Maria will not be coming back to work today after all.

'Oh, that really is a shame,' I say, biting down hard on my tongue because what I really want to say is laced with profanity that will make the man in the doorway blush.

'Perhaps you could come back on Monday? They'll definitely be here then.'

A whole weekend of having to wait? No, that just won't do.

I shake my head. There has to be a better option. *A quicker option.*

'I'm afraid that I'm only in town today. I really don't want to miss them. Would it be possible for you to give me their address so I could visit them at home?'

'Oh, erm, I'm not sure.'

'They will be very happy to see me, I can assure you. We go back years. It's just I can't quite remember where they live, and I'll need to give the address to my driver so he can take me there.' I give my best pathetic smile and a sad tilt of my head. 'Would that be okay?'

The man in the doorway dithers a little more before he is finally of some use.

'I'm not sure I should be giving out their address, but if you're an old friend ...'

I nod encouragingly, hardly daring to speak.

'It's the house at the top of the street on the new development. Meadows Lane, it's called. Your driver won't miss it. It's the biggest one on the street. Amazing place. We all went there last month when William and Maria held a staff barbeque. What a brilliant day. Their garden is massive. You should see the views ...'

His voice trails off as he realises he has just recommended a nice view to a person who doesn't have the benefit of sight.

'Ahh yes, Meadows Lane, I remember now. Don't worry, I'll find it. You have been very kind to me today. What's your name?'

'Jonathan.'

'Well, thank you, Jonathan. I'll be sure to pass on to William and Maria how helpful you have been.'

Jonathan likes the sound of that, and he grins widely as I stand up and carefully make my way out.

We go down in the lift together before separating in the reception area. As I leave the office and relax a little once I'm no longer required to play a character, I think about how my plan has been forced to change.

There would have been some delicious irony in killing William and Maria in the place where the couple effectively 'killed' me, but hurting them in their home won't be such a hardship. Striking them where they feel really safe is an enticing prospect, and as I re-enter the park and remove my wig and glasses, I know that I will no longer be needing a disguise.

Not now I have their address.

Now I can pay them a visit without the need for deception.

Now they will know exactly who is holding the knife as it plunges into them.

So it's goodbye to the office and goodbye to the place where things started to go wrong for me. I didn't fail to notice it on the way out, the meeting room where my world had been turned upside down half a year ago.

How could I forget it?

It's not every day that an innocent person is accused of something terrible.

7

SIX MONTHS EARLIER

DAVID

I'm halfway through my tuna sandwich when the phone rings on my desk. *Typical,* I think as I put my food down and use a napkin to wipe my mouth. I had been looking forward to a lunch break of catching up on the football news online, but I'm barely five minutes into it before I've been interrupted. I knew I should have left the office for lunch or at least gone into the canteen. This serves me right for thinking I could get some peace at my desk. But it's raining outside, so staying in seemed like the more sensible option. But I'm not feeling particularly happy as I pick up my phone and say hello.

And I only feel worse when I hear what the person at the other end of the line has to say.

'Hi, David. It's Becky. Can you come to my office right away, please?'

'Er, yeah, sure. Is everything okay?'

'If you could just come and see me now, please. Thank you.'

That's all Becky says before she hangs up and leaves me staring at the receiver. It hadn't been much, but it hadn't been good. A phone call from the HR manager requesting my immediate presence can't be good, can it?

What is this about? I have absolutely no idea, but I do know that I probably shouldn't leave Becky waiting, so I wrap my sandwich back up and leave it beside my keyboard, hoping that it won't be too long until I'm able to come back and finish it.

How naïve I was. If only I had known then what was about to happen, I would have just finished my sandwich before going to see Becky. It would have been the last meal I enjoyed before everything in my life fell apart.

I knock before entering Becky's office, and she beckons me in before urging me to make sure the door is closed behind me. That's another ominous sign, I think, and as I take my seat opposite her, I take a deep breath.

'There has been a complaint made against you,' Becky begins, only making eye contact for the briefest of moments before looking down at a piece of paper on the desk in front of her.

'A complaint? What is it?'

I try to think of anything I could have done that might have resulted in somebody else here feeling like they had to put a complaint in against me. But I'm friendly with everybody. I'm not rude or demanding. I'm a real team player. *Unless ...*

'Is it about one of my jokes?' I ask, figuring that must be it.

'Your jokes?'

'Yeah, I made a few in the canteen the other day. Nothing bad. Just a bit of harmless fun among colleagues.'

I'm referring to a few jokes I made, but they had been

very tame, all made with the sole intention of lightening the mood amongst my teammates. Even then, I'd only said them to my closest friends here, so surely they wouldn't have complained, would they?

'No, it's not about any jokes,' Becky says, bringing that line of inquiry to an abrupt end.

'Oh, okay. Then what is it?'

'There has been an allegation of misconduct made against you.'

'Misconduct. What do you mean?'

Becky hesitates for a moment before answering.

'Sexual misconduct.'

I can't believe what I'm hearing.

'You're joking, right?'

'I'm afraid not.'

'Sexual misconduct? What are you talking about? Who has said that?'

'Adelina.'

I think of Adelina, an attractive woman in her early thirties whom I have always been on friendly terms with and whom I once asked out for a drink, but she's someone I have definitely never crossed any lines with.

'Adelina? What did she say?'

'She said that you forced yourself on her at the staff party last week.'

'She said *what*?'

'She also said you were aggressive with her and wouldn't take no for an answer,' Becky goes on, reading from the paper that presumably has Adelina's statement on it. 'She said she felt threatened before you eventually left her alone when she made it clear she wasn't interested.'

'This is a joke, right?'

'No, there's nothing funny about this, David.' She gives me a stern look. 'You deny it?'

'Yes, of course I deny it because it didn't happen!'

Becky frowns before consulting the piece of paper again, but I feel like snatching it away from her and throwing it in the bin. Whatever is written on it is clearly rubbish.

'She's lying! I have never forced myself on her or anybody else! You have to believe me!'

'So you're saying she has made it up?'

'Yes!'

'Why would she do that?'

'I don't know, but she has! I don't even know her that well.'

'You two have worked together for eight months, ever since she joined the company.'

'Well, yeah, but we're hardly close.'

'She says you asked her out for a drink once.'

'Yeah, but that's not a crime, is it? And that's all I did.'

'She turned down the offer of a drink. Did you leave it at that, or did you ask her again?'

'I left it at that! God, I'm not some pervert!'

'I didn't say you were.'

'But you're accusing me of harassing a woman.'

'Adelina is making this allegation against you, yes.'

'And do you believe her?'

'It's not about what I believe.'

'Well, I'm telling you it didn't happen, so that's that.'

'I'm afraid it's not as simple as that.'

'What do you mean?'

It's only then that I begin to realise this situation is far worse than I first imagined.

'You know I had to speak to you once before about how much alcohol you consumed at the Christmas party,' Becky reminds me.

'Yeah, I remember. And I said I would tone it down, which I did.'

'A few people at that party thought you were being a little, how can I put it? Lecherous, inappropriately so, around your female colleagues.'

'I was drunk, and I might have been flirting a little bit, but I wasn't lecherous.'

'But you can see why we might consider it a troubling pattern of behaviour now that this more serious allegation has been made?'

'No, I don't.' I raise my hands in a gesture of disbelief. 'I haven't done anything wrong!'

'That's not all.'

'What else?

'I've personally overheard you telling some jokes that could be considered offensive.'

'You said this wasn't about the jokes!'

'It's not, but when taken into account alongside these other behaviours ...'

'Oh come on, I'm just having fun. I don't mean anything by it.'

'That's not how everyone sees it.'

I throw my hands up in the air, more dramatically now, exasperated at how this conversation is going. If anything, it feels less like a conversation and more like an assault on me.

'What's going on here? Can you tell me because I'm struggling to understand? Are you giving me a formal warning?'

Becky finally looks up from her paper, her expression deadly serious.

'Not a warning, no.' Her voice is measured, grave. 'This is formal notice that your employment at Gallagher's Ad Agency is being terminated for failing to comply with the behaviours required of our employees.'

'Excuse me? You're firing me? For what? A bit of flirting and a few rubbish jokes?'

'Have you been listening to what I've told you, David? You

have been accused of sexual harassment. This is serious misconduct.'

'But I didn't do it!' I start to stand, pushing my palms down hard onto the desk in front of me.

'Please, David, stay seated. Calm down.'

'No, I won't calm down. This is crazy! What evidence do you have?'

'We have a written statement from Adelina.'

'It's her word against mine!'

'And we have a pattern of behaviour that could be deemed concerning.'

'It's not a pattern of behaviour. I just had a little too much to drink at a party one night, and I might have made a couple of jokes that could be considered slightly sexist, but I didn't harass anyone, and I have certainly never forced myself on anyone!'

'Mr and Mrs Gallagher would like you to read and sign this.'

Becky opens a drawer beside her desk and takes out another piece of paper. Then she slides it across, allowing me to scan it quickly.

'What is it?'

'It's the termination of your employment. They would like you to sign it so we can process it and both parties can move on.'

'I'm not signing this because I didn't do what you're accusing me of!'

'If you sign it today, then William and Maria have agreed that they will provide you with a reference that does not state the exact reason you left. That will help you find another job. But if you don't sign it, then I'm afraid they will provide no reference. I advise you do as they say.'

'No, I won't. I want to see them first!'

'You know as well as I do, David, that they're not here right now.'

'Because they're in Paris on some business trip? Yeah, I know where they are, probably sipping champagne in a bar overlooking the Eiffel Tower. Well, I don't care. Get them back here so we can discuss this face to face.'

'That's simply not going to happen.'

'Then I'm not signing anything.'

Becky frowns again before pursing her lips and letting out a sigh.

'David, I'm going to talk to you now not as a HR manager but as somebody trying to help another human being. I think you should sign that. You can get the reference, find another job; it doesn't have to be any worse for you than it already is. Trust me, you don't want the real reason for your termination being revealed. I can guarantee nobody will hire you after that.'

'But this isn't right. Aren't I entitled to a fair hearing? I should get my say too.'

'William and Maria have considered all the facts, and they have decided to take this accusation very seriously.'

'Based on what? The word of some woman I once asked out for a drink?'

'No, based on the fact that they were also present at the staff event in question, and what they witnessed backs up Adelina's claims.'

'*What?*'

I'm stunned. Not only am I being accused of something I didn't do, but my bosses are on the side of my accuser.

This isn't right. I know it in my bones. Something more is going on here. It has to be. Why else would they want an innocent man to lose his job?

I'm racking my brains, turning over my options as I sit here in the HR office while Becky tries to persuade me to just sign the form and move on. I consider all the things I could possibly do. File an unfair dismissal claim, for one. I surely have a case. But when I raise that idea with Becky, she just shakes her head sadly and says that it wouldn't get far because Adelina not only has credibility, but she is backed up by credible witnesses in William and Maria. I could get a lawyer and fight this, but it is unlikely I would win, and not only would everyone know what I had been accused of then, but I would also be known as the employee who sued his former bosses, guaranteeing no other boss would ever want me. Not to mention the fact that I haven't exactly got the financial resources for a prolonged legal battle.

So that's why, after another hour of arguing, complaining and pleading, I sign the papers, signalling the end of my time at Gallagher's. Then I leave the HR office and clear my desk, chucking my unfinished sandwich in the bin before bidding the briefest of goodbyes to those nearest to me. Adelina isn't in the office today, just like William and Maria aren't either. *How very bloody convenient*, I think as I take the lift down with my scrappy box of possessions and slam my security pass down at reception.

But, because I haven't seen any of them today, I know I will be seeing them again eventually.

I just don't know when.

8

PRESENT DAY

MARIA

I have to say, this Friday night is shaping up to be far better than I thought it would be when the week began. It's usually at this point, after five gruelling days of work, that I arrive home exhausted and irritable but also well aware that the jobs aren't over yet. There is the children's dinner to make, and trying to satisfy the appetites and ever-changing dietary requirements of two little ones is a full-time job in itself. Then there is the charade of getting them washed and ready for bed, a task that can be fun when they are being cute but that can also be a nightmare when they are being difficult. Once they are settled, that's the point when William will suggest a glass of wine, but I'll have barely made it halfway through the first glass before I feel my eyelids dropping, and before I know it, I've fallen asleep on the sofa.

That's about as wild and fun as my Friday nights usually get.

But this Friday night is different.

After eventually coming to the joint decision to go home straight from the awards ceremony for a quiet night in, just the two of us, I called my mother and asked if she could be so kind as to have Edward and Penny at their place tonight. As expected, she was delighted to have the chance to spend time with her grandchildren before telling me that she thought it was an excellent idea for William and me to have a night to ourselves because, in her words, we 'work far too hard and should take time to enjoy each other's company on occasion'.

I passed that sentiment on to my husband after I'd got off the phone with my mum, and he took it as her suggesting that enjoying each other's company involved something a little sexier than just having dinner together. But I don't like to think of my mum in that way. She is far too proper to be making suggestive remarks about sex. Besides, our parents never had sex, did they? They just opened their front door and there was a baby waiting for them, dropped off by a stork. At least that's what I like to imagine.

With the plan made, I got to break the exciting news to the children that they would be having a sleepover at their grandparents', and they were predictably thrilled. Penny actually did a little dance, bless her. It wasn't quite as easy to persuade them to put what they needed into an overnight bag, but after helping make sure they had the basic necessities like toothbrushes, pyjamas and their favourite sleeping companions, which consisted of teddies and a stack of bedtime stories, they were all set.

Now my parents are at the door, and my two little ones are squealing as I go to answer it.

'Thanks for doing this,' I say to my mum while my dad bends down and takes Penny and Edward in a big hug. He's had bad knees for the last few years, a result of working on a building site carrying heavy loads in his youth, but he still manages to get down low for his grandkids whenever they are near. Perhaps my proudest moment since starting the business with William was the day we were earning enough to pass on some of that wealth to my parents so that they no longer had to work as they aged. Giving back to them after all they did for me when I was younger was a dream come true. I smile as I think how it's certainly helped save my poor dad's knees from deteriorating any further.

I give my old man a hug while my mum takes her turn to greet her grandkids before I hand over their bags and quickly run through any important things they might need to know while the kids are in their care for the next twelve hours or so. Things like what to do if Penny has a nightmare or what to say to Edward if he is still hungry later on and demanding more food before bed, but, as always, I'm forgetting that my parents have extensive childcare experience from their time raising me, so they let me know that they'll figure it out some-how. Then it's time for our goodbyes, and William makes an appearance then, a glass of wine already in his hand and wearing more comfortable attire than the suit he left the house in first thing this morning.

'We owe you guys one,' he says. 'We'll take you out for a meal to say thank you. If you survive the night with these two, that is.'

He ruffles Edward's hair before winking at Penny, and my parents laugh, as warm and receptive to my husband as they've always been ever since I introduced him to them. 'He's a fine young man,' my father said after that first get-together, giving me his seal of approval, not that I ever felt it had been in doubt. 'He's very handsome,' my mum had said, her own view clearly swayed by his looks and not just his confident, pleasant demeanour. Their opinion of the man I have chosen to spend my life with has never changed in all that time, and as far as they are concerned, William is perfect. I know that's not quite the case because after living and working with somebody for such a long time, it's impossible not to notice a few flaws, but, overall, I can't complain.

I definitely landed on my feet with William, and I like to think he didn't do too badly with me either.

'Have fun!' we both cry as we wave our children off, their little bodies bouncing up the driveway as my parents usher them into their car. Then we watch them drive away, smiling at their faces beaming from the back seat before the car leaves our street and a strange silence falls across it.

'Do you hear that?' William asks as we stand in the open doorway. 'Is it? Could it be? Peace and quiet?'

'I think it might be,' I reply, savouring it just as much as he is.

'Come on, let's go and have a drink before your parents change their minds and bring those rascals back.'

William leads me quickly back into our home, and I only half-heartedly push the door to behind us. Right now, my focus is on making sure we have a delicious meal to accompany the lovely wine we are savouring, and the pair of us get to work on preparing a dish.

William chops onions and peppers while I cook the chicken and, hey presto, it's less than thirty minutes later when we are sitting down to a Greek-style meal of chicken gyros with pitta breads and tzatziki.

'We really need to go back to Santorini this year,' William muses as he tears off a bit of his bread and dips it in his sauce. 'It's just a shame we can't go to that adults-only hotel we went to just before we got married.'

'The one with the hunky waiters? Yeah, I'd love to go back there,' I say with a smile.

'I was thinking more for the swim-up pool bar but whatever,' William replies, humouring me.

'You know I only have eyes for you.'

'That's more like it.'

We share a look then, one that threatens to make us forget all about the food on the table and send us scampering into the bedroom to really make the most of having the house to ourselves. Perhaps if we were in our twenties again, then that's exactly what would happen, but we're a little older now and therefore less likely to act purely on lustful whims. We can at least finish our meal, and that's what we do.

I bring up a couple of things from work that have been playing on my mind recently, like whether or not we need to increase the capacity of our accounts team and if it might be worth us hiring a new creative designer to give that particular department a boost. But William has no interest in business chat tonight, and he politely tells me to stop talking about such things before he uses his phone to engage the sound system we have installed in our home.

A simple swipe on the app makes music play from the speakers, and I immediately register that he's picked a good playlist to get us in the mood for what else is to come this evening. It's a song we danced to on that Greek holiday many years ago, and the same song we made sure was played at our wedding. Just hearing it now transports me out of this house in the English countryside and all the way over to the idyllic and sun-kissed town with the pretty white buildings where we first heard this song.

'Great choice,' I tell him as I close my eyes and imagine we're on the other side of Europe right now.

'I always said I could have been a DJ in another life,' William jokes.

'Well, I'm glad you're not. Lots of occupational hazards in that job. Like drugs. And tinnitus.'

'I was thinking more about all the cute women who would come up to my DJ booth with their song requests.'

'Oh, really? That's a little naughty of you.'

'But of course, if I were a DJ, I'd be waiting for you to come and your request. You'd be the only girl I'd want to see.'

We share another look, and this time, there is no chance of either of us going back to our food. We're only hungry for each other now, and as we leave the table and meet in a passionate clinch, a part of me wonders if William is going to suggest we get down to business right here. But then he breaks off from our kiss and scoops me up in his arms, sweeping me off my feet, and I giggle like I'm a blushing bride again.

He carries me out of the dining room and into the hallway in the direction of the stairs, and while I tell him to stop being silly and to put me down before he damages his back, he tells me he is fine and keeps holding me aloft as we ascend.

I glimpse the front door as we go up and notice it's not quite locked, but I'm not going to spoil the mood. I'll just come down and sort it after we're finished in the bedroom. I know I'll be back downstairs anyway to clear away the dinner plates.

But as we reach the upstairs landing and start kissing again, more urgently this time, I have no idea that the pair of us would be going back downstairs shortly for a very different reason.

That front door is about to come back and haunt us.

For ever.

9

DAVID

I might have guessed that William and Maria would live in a house as grand as this one. It makes sense. They are rich, successful businesspeople. They are hardly going to live in squalor, are they? The property in front of me is truly something special, though.

Just like I was told, this is the biggest house on this new development, standing proudly at the top of the street and looking down on all of the other homes here, which are almost as nice but not quite. *Typical of the Gallaghers*, I think. *They always have to be a little bit different.*

A little bit better.

After waiting for the sun to go down before I make my way up the street, I glance in at a few windows as I pass, just to see if people are home and whether or not they might prove to be a problem later. I have work to do, and the last thing I want is to be interrupted by a nosey neighbour who has come to check on a disturbance like William begging for mercy or Maria screaming for help. But some of the homes seem to be empty, an idea backed up by the lack of any vehicles on the driveway, and I figure that most of the people who live here are out enjoying their Friday evening.

But William and Maria are home, and that is all that matters.

I can see the car on their driveway, as well as several lights on around their property as I enter the grounds and find myself a good hiding place in amongst the bushes by a side fence. I watch from there as an elderly couple arrive, and the front door opens before two kids appear, excited and apparently ready for a sleepover if their little bags are anything to go by. Then they say their goodbyes before joining the older couple in their car and waving through the window as they are driven away.

I had anticipated that there might be children present this evening, not that I would have ever entertained hurting them. My gripe is with their guilty parents, so I would have made sure they were safe when I went inside to confront William and Maria. But now they are out of the way, it's one less thing to worry about.

And from what I can see, the couple inside the house have even less to worry about.

I can see them both through the windows, moving around in their 'manor', him with his glass of wine, her with a smile on her face as she prepares a meal before they sit down and dine, talking to each other, laughing, probably flirting, and definitely having a good time.

I feel like even more of a voyeur when I watch William pick his wife up and carry her out of the dining room, and while I lose sight of them then, I guess they have gone upstairs. The passion is clearly alive and well in their relationship, and the pair are obviously making the most of being kid-free for the evening. But I am about to ruin their private party by making my presence known.

The first thing I am going to do is try their front door.

It won't be a big problem if it is locked because I've already seen a couple of open windows around the house, so I will try them next if this point of entry isn't available. But, incredibly, a gentle push on the door shows it to be unlocked, and as I breach the home, I am almost salivating at the prospect of the shock on William's and Maria's faces when they see me.

As I step into the wide hallway, I listen out for any clues as to where the couple are. The soft moaning coming from upstairs gives me my answer, and I shake my head before closing the door behind me as quietly as I can. Knowing that I have a little more time to explore my surroundings while the couple are otherwise engaged, I note the decorative bouquet sitting on a small table by the side of the staircase, something that provides a pleasant welcome to anybody who enters this home.

I find many more examples of similar classy touches as I move deeper into the house, and it's clear that at least one of William or Maria is house-proud from how tidy and orderly the place is. I consider that the couple might have a house-keeper who maintains this place while they are busy at the office, but I also remember that the pair always advocated cleanliness and orderliness in the workplace, so it could just be them who's responsible for making this place so pristine.

The only evidence that anything is out of place is in the kitchen and dining room, where the meal has been prepared and then half eaten. The plates are still sitting on the table beside the glasses of wine, while there is a pan in the kitchen with leftover chicken in, allowing me to dip my finger in and try a little of the sauce that has been made to complement the dish.

It's tasty, with an unmistakable air of quality, just like I assume the wine will be. But I don't allow myself a sip of that. I need a clear head for what is to come.

Returning to the hallway, I pause so I can better hear what is going on above me. But the sounds have ceased, and that suggests the couple have finished what they are doing in the bedroom. Now are they going to come back downstairs tonight?

Or will I have to go up there and surprise them?

Pulling the knife out from where it is tucked into my waistband, I grip the handle and ponder my next move. It's then that I spot a glass trophy sitting on a windowsill in the hallway, and I pick it up to examine it further.

Best Business Award 2022

I realise this must be what the couple won today. No wonder they didn't come back to the office. They must have been celebrating all afternoon.

Huh.

I feel like throwing the award against the wall. But that would give away my position, so I have no choice but to return it to where I found it. Then I turn my attention to the staircase.

The thought of catching the pair in a state of post-coital undress up there, tangled beneath their bedsheets, is certainly amusing, but I know now that I will enjoy an element of surprise regardless of where I confront them. But it has been a long day for me, made far longer by the fact that the couple were not in the office this afternoon as they should have been, so I start to climb the staircase to speed things up.

I'm too impatient to wait any longer.

By this time of today, if it had gone as planned, I fully

expected to be in police custody for crimes committed against the Gallaghers. They should already be dead by now, and I should be in handcuffs, or at least on the run, trying to evade the law – although that surely wouldn't have lasted long. As it is, I am still an innocent man as I climb the stairs, innocent in more ways than one, and William and Maria are still breathing in oxygen, probably dreaming about sales targets and balance sheets and whether or not to holiday in Cannes this year.

As I reach the top of the stairs, I count five doors up here. The nearest one to me is open, and I can see the rim of a large bathtub as well as a sink and shelf full of men's toiletries. The next door appears to lead into a dressing room, and I catch sight of Maria's extensive make-up inventory as well as one open wardrobe door that reveals an array of luxurious dresses, sure to be worn for all the important functions she has to attend.

Creeping across the soft carpet, careful not to make a sound but aware that I could be about to tread across a creaky floorboard at any second, I hear the couple talking in low voices from behind the closed door at the end of the hallway. But before I get there, I pass two more rooms, which clearly belong to the children. One is pink and packed with dolls, teddies and a large mural of a graceful unicorn jumping over a rainbow. The other bedroom is painted a jungly green and full of dinosaur books, magazines, figurines and posters.

I consider for a moment what it must be like to grow up with parents like William and Maria. Their children surely want for nothing, which is great for them, but means there is a very thin line for the parents to tread to ensure they don't grow up spoiled and entitled. My own upbringing was a little different to what I imagine the children in this house experience, and while I never struggled or felt unloved by those who raised me, I was always aware that other children in society had more than me. I recognised from an early age that there are different levels to life, levels that I struggled to ascend to even when I became an adult and had more power to try to do something about what might be felt as inequalities.

But then again, there is more to life than having money. Things like family and friends. Treating others how you wish to be treated. Making the world a better place. Giving back without expecting anything in return. I know that while I'm not as wealthy as the Gallaghers – and most likely never will be – I am a far better person than any of them.

I have morals.

But I also have this knife in my hand, and that means, for one night only, I am going to cease being the perfect citizen I have been all my life and do something drastically different.

I am almost at the closed bedroom door when I hear the sound of footsteps approaching and realise that somebody has got out of bed and is now heading in my direction.

Have they heard me? No, I've been quiet, and besides, they probably would have called out if they suspected somebody was in their home. But they are getting closer, and I know it is only a matter of time until the bedroom door opens …

And then, whoever comes through it will see me and the knife in my hand.

So this is it. My moment. My chance to make them pay.

I hold the knife out and prepare to drive forward as soon as that door opens.

One thing is for sure; whoever it is will meet a grisly end.

And then I inadvertently put my weight on what turns out to be a creaky floorboard.

I can tell immediately that those in the bedroom have stopped what they are doing.

There's a long pause.

'Did you hear that?'

It's Maria's voice.

I hold my breath, terrified that I've just lost my best ally, *surprise.*

'What?'

That's William's voice, and it was a little farther away, making me think that he is still lying on the bed while his wife almost encountered my knife first.

'It sounds like somebody is out in the hallway,' Maria says.

'There's nobody here.'

'But I heard something.'

'It's probably just the wind. Unless your parents have had enough of the kids already and dropped them back off. But I think they'd be making a little more noise than that.'

I wait to see what happens next.

Will Maria leave the room and meet me head-on? Or will I have to go in there myself?

Then I see the handle on the bedroom door begin to turn.

Somebody is coming out.

And I know precisely how to play this now.

10

MARIA

I open the bedroom door and peer out, checking to see if anybody is there because I'm sure I just heard a noise. What am I expecting to see? A masked villain with a deadly weapon? If so, then I have absolutely no idea what the point of me checking is because I'd be completely helpless in that situation.

But there is nobody there. Everything looks perfectly normal.

'So who is it?' my husband asks. 'Are we being burgled or not?'

William chuckles, and I look back at him lying on the bed, clearly not finding this situation as worrying as I did a moment ago. He's basking in the afterglow of sex, and his cheeks are still flushed as he lies there running a contented hand over his chest hair. I look at his otherwise smooth, near flawless body. I would have still been lying there beside him

feeling equally as smug if I hadn't needed to visit the bathroom and then heard the floorboard creak.

'It's probably just the house shifting,' William suggests
after he notices that I still look a little worried. 'Houses do
that, you know.'

'Yeah, old houses. But this is a new one.'

'Well, maybe we're the ones who shifted it.'

William winks at me then, clearly feeling pleased with
himself and the performance he just gave, and I can't help
but laugh.

'It was good, but it wasn't so good as to make the founda-
tions move,' I tell him, bursting his bubble slightly, but he
knows I'm only teasing him.

'How about we go downstairs and tidy up; then we can
finish that bottle of wine,' he suggests, and I tell him that
sounds like a good idea before I leave the bedroom and head
for the bathroom.

Turning on the light, I make my way over to the toilet, the
cotton slip I put on just after getting out of bed floating
against my bare legs and tickling me slightly, but in a nice
way. And then I steal a glance at myself in the mirror as I
pass it.

That's the exact moment when I see who is standing
behind me.

A hand goes over my mouth before I can scream, and
then the cold blade of a knife is against my throat, further
dissuading me from making a sound. I stare at my horrified
reflection in the mirror, the one that shows me being held
captive while a man holds me tightly, his arms around my
torso, my mouth covered, my neck vulnerable.

And then he whispers in my ear.

'Stay quiet, or I will kill you. Now, let's go and see your
husband.'

I want to speak. I want to ask David why he is doing this.

I know his name because I never forget my old employees. I could name every person who has ever worked at Gallagher's because they're all important to me. They were all part of my team. But David is more memorable than most because of how he left our company.

He's the first person who left it under a cloud.

But I don't say anything because I'm going to follow his rules. He's told me to stay quiet, so I will. I hope by doing so, he won't hurt me. But what is his plan here? Why is he in our house?

And how did he get in?

I think of the front door as he leads me out of the bathroom. How I didn't make sure it was properly shut after saying goodbye to the children. How I neglected it before dinner and again before coming up here with William. How I thought everything would be okay, that we'd get away with being a little bit lax for once, because this is a safe neighbourhood.

What an idiot.

I've made it easy for an intruder. And now they are in, anything could happen.

David pushes me onwards in the direction of the bedroom, and my bare feet scurry across the carpet as I try to keep the pace he's insisting on. I can hear William whistling as we get nearer. All is still all right with the world; he's oblivious to the danger we are in.

But, just like me, he is about to get the shock of his life.

'I was thinking we could take the kids to the beach on Sunday,' he calls out as David and I reach the doorway. He's sitting on the edge of the bed and pulling a T-shirt over his head, his back to us. 'The weather looks good. We could get ice creams. Maybe fish and chips to eat on the sea wall. What do you think?'

I wish I could tell him that sounds like a lovely idea and

that the kids would love it too. But I can't. All I can do is stand helplessly in the doorway.

And then my captor speeds things up.

'I don't think you'll be going to the beach on Sunday,' David says, and William spins around at the sound of his voice, almost falling off the bed as he gets to his feet, moving more urgently than I've ever seen before.

His terror is evident in his eyes when he realises the peril I am in. Then I watch the shock register on his face when he too recognises who it is who's here in our home.

'David?' he cries. 'What the hell are you doing?'

'What does it look like I'm doing?' David retorts. 'I'm holding a knife to your wife's throat, and I'm thinking about spilling her blood all over this lovely carpet of yours.'

The bile surges in my throat, and I feel like I'm about to vomit. I actually think of how that would play out considering the hand over my mouth. Would I have to choke it back, or would David remove his hand in disgust once he realised what was happening? It might not be such a bad thing if it makes him release his grip on me, but while my nausea is strong, I don't quite bring up my dinner yet.

But there's still a chance, depending on how this goes.

'Why?' William asks, one hand out towards us as if he can somehow control this situation. But he can't because the only person in control here is the man with the knife.

'What do you mean why?' David snarls, his mouth so close to my right ear that his words seem almost deafening.

'Why are you doing this?'

'Why do you think?'

I watch William try to figure it out, but he looks unsure. I am too. I mean, we both know that we fired David after we believed he was guilty of sexual harassment. But that can't be what this is about, surely? I mean, we had no choice but to fire him. He can't blame us for that, can he?

'Is this about what happened with Adelina?' William asks, referencing the woman whose complaint against David ultimately led to his dismissal.

'That's part of it, yes. It's also about the fact that you forced me out without giving me a fair hearing. You've ruined my life. Both of you. So now I'm here to ruin yours.'

This really doesn't feel good. I can't imagine how there's going to be a way for us to get out of this. But that doesn't stop my husband trying.

'Okay, I hear you. So let's just talk about this, okay?'

'Why should we? You didn't let me talk about it when you fired me. You didn't let me defend myself like you want to defend yourself now. You weren't even there. You were in Paris on some business trip. You probably weren't even working. You were probably taking selfies on the Champs-Élysées or fooling around in your hotel room, all while my life was being deliberately dismantled back at the office.'

'Please, David. Just let my wife go. You're scaring her.'

'Oh, am I? I'm so sorry. How about if I do this?'

I feel David press the blade firmer against my neck as his arms squeeze me even tighter, and I brace myself.

Will it hurt when he slices my throat open? Will I feel my arteries burst? And will I see my own blood spill as I fall to the floor before my eyes inevitably close and I lose my grip on life, never to see the faces of my precious children again?

'No, stop! Please!'

William is begging David, my husband's hands together now as if in prayer. I've never seen him look so afraid. So out of his depth. *So helpless.*

It makes no difference. David grips me in this perilous position. But I'm still alive. He hasn't killed me yet. Maybe he won't. Maybe I can get out of this. Maybe I can hug my children again and live to see them grow. But right now it feels like I'll need a miracle for that to happen.

'Why did you do it?' David demands. 'Why did you ruin me? What had I ever done to deserve what you did to me?'

'David, please. Just put the knife down, and then we'll talk.'

'We're talking now! So answer me!'

'We didn't ruin you. We were just following protocols. Adelina made the claim against you. You harassed her. What else were we supposed to do? We had to act.'

'I never touched her! I never harassed her! She was lying, and you two believed her!'

'David, please, the evidence ...'

'There was no evidence! You just made me sign that form, and then I was gone, as if I'd never even set foot in that build-ing. As if I hadn't tried my best every single day that I was there. Do you have any idea what my life has been like since that day?'

'We gave you a reference. We gave you a chance to get another job. We didn't have to do that.'

'Oh, so that makes it okay, does it? That excuses you from firing an innocent employee? What did you think? That I would just move on without harbouring some kind of resent-ment? That I would just forget all about the injustice of it? That it would be that easy for me to start again, to explain to my partner why I had to find a new job? Really?' I feel him pause for breath, his voice almost catching. 'It was a night-mare, and it's a nightmare that still hasn't ended for me.'

'I'm sorry, David. I really am, but –'

'No, you're not sorry. Not for me, anyway. The only thing you're sorry about is the fact that your cosy Friday night in with your wife has been ruined. Well, that's not all that is going to be ruined by the time this night is over.'

'David, please, listen to me.'

'No, you listen to me. I've lost everything since that day you fired me. I told my partner what happened. I was honest with her, like a decent man should be. I told her how there had been a false claim made against me and that I had been dismissed without a proper investigation. I thought I was doing the right thing. But do you know what she did? She left me!'

'I'm very sorry about that.'

'No, you're not! Stop insulting me with your lies! You're only sorry because your wife is in danger. Well, get used to that feeling because this is not over yet. Not by a long way.'

That's when David removes his hand from over my mouth, relieving some of the pressure on me although the knife is still very much in position on my neck. Then he uses his free hand to take something out of his back pocket.

It's a pair of handcuffs.

He wants my husband to put them on.

11

MARIA

I watch as my husband reluctantly wraps the handcuffs around his wrists and then seals them shut. I hear the mechanism click before he holds his hands up to show David that he has done as he's been told.

'Good, now you're going to get a little taste of what it feels like to lose control,' David says. 'Okay, Maria, your turn.'

I feel my captor loosen his grip on me as he takes out the handcuffs meant for me. But with his attention momentarily elsewhere other than the knife at my neck, I seize my chance.

Throwing my head back to where I know David's head will be, I feel our skulls collide, and while it hurts me, it definitely hurts him more. I hear him cry out in pain and shock and fury before he staggers backwards, the knife falling as he holds his head and checks for blood.

Now we have some separation, I can make a run for it before I get handcuffed too.

But I need William with me.

'Come on!' I urge my husband, and despite what we know to be an incredible risk, we take what might be our one and only opportunity to escape this mess and sprint out of the bedroom while David is still dazed, hoping we can make it downstairs and out the front door before he catches us.

I'm leading the way, my adrenaline pumping and heart rate spiking, most likely operating in some state of heightened shock that a thing like this has happened to us. Ten minutes ago, this was the perfect Friday night. Now it feels like I'm a character in a horror film, running for the exits before the lunatic with the knife can catch me and condemn me to being yet another victim who simply wasn't smart enough to get away.

But this is no film. It's real life. No writer has already ordained if I will live or die. This is all up to me and the man running just behind me. My husband and I can get out of this if we're desperate enough, and as we run down the stairs, I have a feeling that we are.

Then I hear William cry out, and as I turn around, I see him falling, his eyes desperate with fear, unable to properly cushion his fall because of the handcuffs on his wrists.

I try my best to soften his landing by putting my hands out to catch him, but it's no good. I can't quite reach him, and he tumbles down the stairs helplessly, although I do manage to swerve to avoid being wiped out by his falling body.

We're both at the bottom of the stairs now, me on my feet and William in a crumpled heap, and I crouch down quickly to check he's okay. He's clearly a little sore, but he'll live, or at least he will if I can get him up on his feet and on the move again.

'You're okay, yeah? We must go!' I'm pulling at William, trying to lift him to his feet, constantly aware that we're losing precious time in the process.

As I help William up, I know we're only a few yards away from the front door, and once we're outside, we can take refuge in the darkness of our garden, somewhere our tormentor won't find us. He'll surely panic and give up, running away before we can call the police.

And then we'll have survived this ordeal, we'll live another day, and we'll see our children again.

It's not a useful thought, but I imagine I'll need some kind of therapy after this. Some specialist who deals in trauma to talk to me about how best to process the shock and move on with my life without being haunted by this horror for the rest of it. I could have nightmares. It's not every day a person gets threatened at knifepoint, especially in their own home. Oh God, what if I am never able to enjoy this house like I did before? Are we going to have to move? The home I've been so happy to raise my kids in is tainted now, so maybe.

But I'm getting way ahead of myself.

First things first, I have to make sure I live to even have the luxury of problems like those.

'You stupid bitch! Get back here!'

I instinctively glance up to see David at the top of the stairs, a smear of blood on his forehead where our skulls met with such force.

He looks angry. Very, very angry. He also has the knife in his hand.

Damn it, why didn't I just pick it up when I had the chance?

'Come on!' I grab William, and we rush towards the door. I can hear David descending the stairs rapidly, his feet hammering as he closes the gap between us.

Reaching for the door handle, I turn it and feel the cool evening air seep into this hot house, and it's a sign that we're almost free now. If we can just make it up the driveway and away from the lights of our home, David won't be able to find us …

I hear William groan, and I turn to see him buckled over, as if he's been punched in the stomach. He must have turned back to hold off David while I made my escape, but without the use of his hands, he was powerless to defend himself, and now he is down again. To add to the nightmare, David now has the knife to my husband's throat. Even though I could technically get away, how am I supposed to leave the man I married?

'Take one step out that door and he dies,' David declares, and his voice is as chilling as if he genuinely doesn't care what happens next.

'Just go!' William cries. 'Get the hell out of here!'

He's being brave. He's willing to sacrifice himself to let me escape. But I'm not willing to lose him. We both have to get out of here. That's non-negotiable.

'Stop!' I step away from the open door. 'I won't run. But only if you tell us what you want.'

I'm giving David a chance here. A chance to hopefully reach some sort of agreement. A chance to end this without any real bloodshed.

'I want you to clear my name,' David says, and even though he's in a position of power with my husband, I detect a weakness in him. It's evident that what happened to him has pushed him to the brink, and even though what he is doing here is unforgivable, I have to believe that he is not really a callous or crazy man. He certainly wasn't like this when I knew him in the office. He's just backed himself into a corner. But there can be a way out.

'Tell us what you want us to do. Whatever it is, we'll do it,' I say, holding my hands out towards him. 'Don't hurt us. It's not worth it. You won't just be destroying our lives. You'll destroy yours as well. And theirs.'

I gesture to a studio photo on the wall of my children, and David looks at it, seeing their two young smiling faces, how they look so happy with their parents' arms wrapped around them. He has to know that they need the pair of us, and therefore, he has to know that he can't hurt us, right?

'Maria, run!' William shouts. The knife is still perilously close to his skin, but he's clearly not willing to take any chances if one of us can get away.

But I don't go anywhere. I'm starting to feel more and more confident that we can find a peaceful resolution for all this, and that won't involve me running away without my husband.

'Close the door,' David instructs me. 'Then we'll talk.'

'Okay, I can do that,' I tell him, and while William continues to protest, I shut the front door. I'm letting David know that I'm willing to keep this civil.

'In the dining room, now,' David says, and I do just that while he follows me, shepherding William at knifepoint.

It shouldn't be a surprise, but I find it hard to understand how things can be exactly as we left them. There's food on our plates and wine in our glasses. It wasn't so long ago that my biggest problem this evening was getting the sauce just right for the chicken.

Oh, to have simple problems like that again.

'Handcuffs,' David says, and he tosses me the pair he wanted me to put on when we were upstairs.

I can't see a way to avoid us both being in restraints, so I placidly do as I'm told. David makes William take a seat at the table beside me. Then he sits down opposite us, placing the knife beside the plate I was eating from earlier. There is a brief moment of silence before he speaks again.

'You know, I set out this morning with the sole purpose of killing you both,' he tells us as calmly as if we were in a business meeting together. 'I went to your office first, but you weren't there. I heard you were at an awards show. How did that go for you?'

William and I share a look because neither of us is sure if it's wise to mention the success of this afternoon, but it seems we don't need to. David knows anyway.

'You won, didn't you? Yeah, that sounds about right. Because you two always win, don't you? In business. In love. In life. Look at you, you've got it all.'

'So. You're jealous. That's what this is about, isn't it?' William says, an edge to his voice. I wish he hadn't, though, because antagonising the dangerous man who seems to have calmed down a little bit hardly seems like the best idea. 'You're not clever or hard-working enough to achieve the things we have, so you react like this, screaming out at the world instead of taking responsibility for your actions and realising that you get out of this life exactly what you put into it.'

'William,' I say sternly to shut him up, my tone like that of a mother scolding her child.

But it's no good. He's off on a rant now, whether driven by fear or disgust I can't quite imagine.

'People like you disgust me. Can you imagine a world where everybody reacted to the cards life deals like you have done? If instead of addressing our problems by trying to better ourselves, we just grabbed a weapon and started threatening people? Where would we all be then?'

'William, please,' I try again before glancing nervously at David to see how he is taking this lecture. Not very well, I imagine. But to my surprise, he has a smirk on his face.

'Like I said, I set out this morning with the sole purpose of killing you both,' he says. 'But now I've realised that will be making things far too easy for you. I need you to suffer more than that, and the only way I can make that happen is to have you around so you can feel what it's like to lose control of your life like I lost control of mine.'

'What do you mean?' I can't help but ask him.

'I want you both to admit that you made a mistake. I want my termination to be recognised as unfair dismissal and financial damages to be awarded, along with the significant damages to your reputation that your company will incur from admitting such a thing. And then I want you both to step down from your positions in your company, so you will know precisely how I felt when I lost a job I loved against my wishes.'

'Get real,' William scoffs. 'That's not going to happen. None of it is.'

'Okay. In that case, I'll just wait here until your children come home, and then we'll see how that goes for you all,' David says coldly.

'Wait,' I say, sick with fear, cutting him off before he can say anything else about my children. And then I have a thought; it's a nasty one, but I'm desperate. 'If the harassment claim was false, why have you come to us? Why haven't you gone to Adelina? She's the one who accused you.'

'Don't you think I already tried that,' David tells me as he rolls his eyes. 'But I couldn't find her. I heard a rumour that she went home to Albania after having left your company, which again, is interesting because why would she suddenly quit not just her job but the UK if she was genuinely the victim?'

'Unfortunately, she left because – sadly – she couldn't move on from what happened while she was working with us,' William interrupts. 'It makes perfect sense that she would feel like she needed a fresh start or, in her case, the familiarity of home.'

'That might be how somebody wanted it to look,' David replies calmly, as if he has thought of every possibility. 'But I know something else happened. Adelina isn't here to tell me about it, only you two are. So that's why I'm here. And that's why you're going to tell me everything from the beginning, starting with when you first heard the claim and how you ended up deciding I was guilty of something I didn't do.'

And that's when William falls uncharacteristically quiet.

So I fill the silence for him.

I have no choice but to recall the day when I first heard that my perfect company wasn't so perfect after all.

12

MARIA

I t's payday, so there's even more of a buzz around the office than usual. I never fail to notice the extra spring in my colleagues' steps at this time of the month when money has been withdrawn from the company bank account and deposited into theirs. I'd like to think that everybody has chosen to work here for their career advancement as well as the opportunity to be in such a vibrant and positive office culture, but I'm not an idiot. I know people only really go to work for money, which is okay, because money makes the world go round, and it certainly helps keep my company afloat.

Not only is everybody moving with a little more energy today now that their bank balances are significantly healthier, but they are louder too, chattering away at their desks or in the canteen, excitedly talking through a few of the plans they have on how to spend their hard-earned cash. I've heard mentions of all sorts this morning, from people planning weekend shopping sprees to a few who are hoping to book a summer holiday soon. Of course, they are free to do whatever they like with their income as long as they continue to put in the effort here, and they are all doing just that.

The good vibes in the office are one of the factors creating my good mood this morning. I've also just had an email from a client who has complimented us on the work we have done for them before promising plenty more work to come our way in the future. That's great news and further proof of the productive team William and I have established here.

And then, out of the blue, my day is soured by some bad news, which also comes in the form of an email, though in this case, it is from our HR manager, Becky.

I see the subject line in my inbox, and instantly my heart sinks.

Notice to Management Committee: Employee Complaint.

With a team of six on the company's management committee, including myself, William, Becky and a few other heads of department, it's not unusual for us to receive notices amongst ourselves. After all, we meet on a weekly basis to discuss anything and everything to do with the business, so we always have plenty of correspondence. But what is unusual is what this particular correspondence refers to.

An employee complaint? That is immediately troubling, so I open the email to learn more.

Becky has called for a meeting to discuss a recent sexual harassment complaint that has been made against another member of staff, and while she doesn't name either party, because protocol requires us to only discuss that in the meeting, it is clear this is a very serious matter.

Having worked so hard to not only make this a profitable

workplace but a safe one too, it seems there has been a significant breach of safeguarding somewhere, and now I am worried about what one of my employees might have suffered. That's why I waste no time in picking up the phone and calling my husband, who will have hopefully seen the email too by now and be able to shed a little more light on this.

Although he's not at his desk with me in our sixth-floor office, I know he is in the building, and I want to see him immediately, so I ask him to come to me as quickly as he can. He doesn't sound too troubled when he answers the phone, so I'm guessing he hasn't read the email yet, but he's on his way up, and I plan to tell him our problem as soon as he gets here. Because, make no mistake, an allegation like this is a big problem for any company.

I don't know the full facts yet, but I don't have to to realise that this could be a disaster for us both internally and externally. Depending on the extent and the severity of the claim, we could not only be looking at a major issue in the workplace but one that might reach further than a single isolated incident. That would be devastating to the environment here and could see management facing a lot of questions from the staff. But if this got out into the wider world, it could give our company a bad reputation, not only within the industry, ruining our chances with potential clients, but also in the eyes of investors, affecting our future plans to increase capital and value by selling shares, by going public on the stock market.

It's easy to overreact, and I'm trying not to, because while this is bad, it might turn out to be a false, unsubstantiated claim. But it's vital to take it extremely seriously so we can get this properly actioned as quickly as possible. Before things get any worse than they might already be.

'What's up?' William asks casually as he saunters into our

office with an apple in his hand. I'm guessing he grabbed that from the fruit bowl in the seating area, the one I suggested we put there so our staff could help themselves to a nutritious snack whenever they felt like it. It's just one of the many benefits we like to offer our employees. But now it seems there could be a downside to working here, one that no amount of free fruit bowls could make up for.

I make sure the door is firmly shut behind him before I start. 'Have you seen Becky's email?' There's no point pussy-footing about. 'One of our employees has made a claim of sexual harassment.'

William quickly checks his inbox, and I wait impatiently for a second for him to catch up to me. But he's taking too long staring blankly at his phone, so I spell it out for him instead.

'This is a crisis. We need to have a meeting right now. I'll summon the other board members. They should all be in the office by now.'

I'm just about to start calling round to gather us all together when William stops me.

'Look, you're right, we do need to have a meeting about this. But calm down a little bit first.'

'Calm down?' I can't fathom his attitude at all. 'One of your employees has been harassed! We need to know who. We need to know what's happened!'

'I know who it is.'

'What?'

'I know who has made the claim. I saw Becky earlier, and she mentioned that she was going to send an email out.'

'Well, thanks for letting me know. So spill the beans.'

'It's Adelina.'

I think of the sales assistant we hired, the one who was so direct and positive in her interview. I remember how we talked about her suitability for the role but also a little bit about her personal life. Like how she had moved to the UK from her homeland of Albania a couple of years earlier and had worked hard to pursue her dream of a career in advertising sales. She was, and as far as I know still is, a confident and dedicated woman, not to mention one who certainly possessed a steely, resourceful spirit. Neither myself nor William needed too long to consider whether or not to hire her because it had been obvious that she would make a welcome addition to our team, and so it had proven ever since she came on board. She always appeared happy here, and I know that her manager, Derek, one of the members of the management committee, has been happy with her performance too.

So this news that she is claiming to have been harassed comes as a total shock.

But my personal and professional instincts give me no reason not to believe her implicitly.

'Oh my God. Is she okay?' I cry.

'Look, she's fine. Well, not fine, but there's no need to panic.'

'Who's the allegation against?'

'We'll discuss it all –'

'William, who is it?' I cut him off. 'You must tell me. I can't go into that meeting not knowing if you do.'

'It's David.'

'David?'

I'm again taken back to the interview process, this time the day I sat across a desk from David Hendricks, a polite and presentable young man who gave me a rundown of his employment history before making me laugh with his sly sense of humour. But it seems there's another side to him that not everybody appreciates. Or at least not Adelina.

'What did he do?'

'He got a bit heavy with her at that staff drinks gathering

last month. Tried it on. Wouldn't take no for an answer, apparently. He'd obviously had too much to drink.'

'That doesn't excuse it!'

'I know. And we both know that this isn't the first time he's overindulged at a work event and got himself into a bother with a colleague.'

William is referring to a time when David had flirted quite openly with several staff members during one of our parties. But there is a big difference between some consensual flirting and harassment.

'We need to speak to him. And Adelina. We need the full story.'

'Yes, we do, and we will. Let's speak with the other managers, and then we'll work through this properly, in accordance with our policy guidelines. And obviously, in the meantime, this needs to be kept quiet.'

'Of course.'

'Okay, let's have the meeting. I'll round up the troops. See you in the boardroom in ten minutes?'

I nod as William walks confidently out of our office. I wish I could stay as composed as he does in times of crisis. Usually I am much more level-headed with work issues, but this is very different. Whatever has happened between Adelina and David needs to be resolved and quickly. We need to determine whether David is guilty.

And if he is, there can only be one outcome.

13

MARIA

'We followed protocols,' I assure David, rubbing my cuffed wrists at our incongruous dining table conference. 'We had the managers meeting, and we considered the content of the allegation before we came to our decision.'

'A decision that was made without even speaking to me?' David snarls. There's so much anger in his eyes that I wonder how this man could ever have charmed me into giving him a job. 'And how exactly is that fair?'

'We didn't need to speak to you,' William cuts in. 'Not once we'd heard what you did to Adelina. Pressuring her for sex. Threatening her when she said no. You're lucky it was nothing more serious than a harassment claim. Your actions could have easily escalated it from a workplace issue to a matter for the police.'

'Here you go again, believing her word over mine. Whatever Adelina claims simply did not happen. She's a liar! Why would you assume my guilt without asking any more questions?'

'We didn't need to. You had demonstrated a clear pattern of behaviour since we first employed you,' my husband goes on. 'We all know what you were like after a few too many drinks. You went after every single woman in the office. Hell, you even dared to try it on with my wife.'

I shudder slightly, but can't help defending David a little here. 'I wouldn't say he tried it on,' I say, although I know I'm not helping by contradicting my husband here. 'But you did cross the line with how flirtatious you were with me at our Christmas party. I admit I did consider giving you a warning afterwards, and once I'd heard Adelina's story, I regretted not doing so.'

'Okay, so I'm a bit flirty after a beer or two,' David says with a shrug, his eyes indifferent. 'But I have never forced myself on a woman, and I definitely didn't deserve to lose everything just because someone chose to make a false claim about me.'

'Well, it's happened,' William says very unsympathetically, 'and I think we all need to move on.'

But unfortunately this isn't the time for him to treat David like a simple item on an agenda. This situation requires more tact. More compassion. More strategic thinking.

More ...

And then I glimpse a way out.

Maybe William is right, or at least his methods are. Let's try to keep this businesslike.

'How much do you want to leave us alone?' I ask calmly.

Both David and my husband seem surprised at what I've just said, but I repeat it.

'We have money, which you obviously know, and while I'm not convinced we have done anything wrong, I can see that we should have spoken to you before we let you go. That would have been the decent thing to do, regardless of whether we were in the office that day or not. So, to make up for it, how about we offer some reparation now?' I pause, looking about the table as if this surreal encounter were a quotidian business meeting. 'What's your thinking? What are you asking for in order to leave us alone?'

I've never been one to believe a problem can be solved simply by throwing money at it, but maybe this is the time to change that view. But, unsurprisingly, William doesn't seem to agree with me.

'What are you on?' my husband hisses. 'This man threatens us with a knife in our own home, and now you want to pay him for the honour?'

I'm just about to whisper my reasoning when David interrupts me.

'You two are hilarious. Here you are, William, the man of the house, who is so up his own arse that he can't even acknowledge he might have made a mistake with a former employee. And look at you, Mrs Perfect, thinking you can just breadcrumb me some of your riches and that's all it'll take to send me scurrying away back to whatever hole you think I crawled out of. You're both seriously deluded, but you, Maria, are the worst.'

'Excuse me?'

'I'm not some minor problem you can just make go away with a suitcase of cash. You can't pay me off.' He stops, looks me straight in the eye. 'You can't pay me off like you paid off Adelina.'

I recoil from the intensity of his gaze. After everything that has happened tonight, that last sentence feels the most shocking.

'What are you talking about?' I ask, baffled. 'We haven't given Adelina any money.'

'Oh, really? So you wouldn't say that £50,000 transferred from your business account to hers is *giving her money*? What would you call it, then? It looks a lot like a pay-off from where I'm sitting.'

I have absolutely no idea what David is talking about, and I look to William, expecting him to look equally surprised. But he doesn't, and David seems to know why.

'You didn't think I'd find out about it, did you?' David chuckles nastily. 'But guess what, I did. And now that I know, it makes me even more convinced that you two have done something wrong.'

'William?' I'm waiting for my husband to say something. *Anything*. 'What does he mean?'

'How do you know about that?' he asks David, and that's not quite what I was hoping he would say.

Has he just confirmed that it actually happened?

'Let's just say I'm still on friendly terms with one of your employees,' David replies. 'I'm not going to name any names because I don't want them to get in trouble, but they told me they'd seen the transaction, so I know it's true.'

'So somebody in our accounts team told you,' William fires back. 'That narrows it down a little, and when I find out who, I'll make sure they'll be joining you at the job centre next week.'

But my husband seems to be missing the point here. Instead of worrying about who has been feeding David confidential information regarding our accounts, he should be worrying about why it is that I have absolutely no information about any such payment myself.

'What is going on?' I cry. 'Why did you give Adelina so much money?'

William looks down at his cuffed hands. 'It was nothing,' he says. 'Simply a bonus.'

'A *bonus*? But only management are entitled to bonuses!'

'That's what I thought,' David chips in. 'Which makes it rather interesting that somebody who isn't a manager managed to get one.'

'William? What is going on?' I demand, feeling more uneasy by the second. The murkier this gets, the more I'm starting to worry that David might be justified in being here this evening, and that's not something I ever imagined I would think when he had the knife to my throat only a few moments ago.

'Okay, it wasn't exactly a bonus,' William admits.

'Go on!' I insist, wondering at the absurdity of being so furious with my husband in this situation.

'It was a payment to ensure Adelina stayed quiet once she made it clear she wanted to leave the company. I couldn't risk her telling anybody about the harassment, particularly because it happened in the workplace. It could have destroyed our reputation, so we agreed on a little incentive.'

'A *little* incentive? Since when does fifty grand count as a little anything!'

'I agree with your wife,' David says with a mournful shake of his head. 'Fifty K is an awful lot of money. I'd say it feels like a cover-up payment. Like a cover-up for the fact she lied. Like a cover-up for the fact you fired an innocent employee. And who knows what else. A cover-up for a whole lot of guilt? It might seem like a lot of money to us, but maybe it was money well spent for you, William, especially if you've kept it a secret from your wife. So what's it really about?'

'I just told you. I didn't want the company's reputation tarnished. I didn't want prospective employees or clients to give us a wide berth.'

David scoffs in disdain at that.

But I have a question of my own.

'William, why didn't you tell me about this?'

'It wasn't really a big deal,' he says, but I'm unconvinced by his offhand tone. 'I just made a business call.'

'But we make all the calls together.'

'Come on, Maria. I did what I thought was best for the company.'

'You had no right! You should have run it by me and the other managers. You needed our approval.'

'Oh, I'm sure that there isn't much that William needs approval for,' David cuts in. 'You're the big boss, aren't you? You can do anything you want. Even lie to your wife.'

'Shut up,' William snaps, seeming to forget that he is talking to a man who not long ago was pressing a knife into the soft skin of his neck.

'So,' David starts, getting back to business, 'just to clarify: you genuinely had no idea about this, Maria?'

'No, I did not.'

'Interesting.'

'Is it?' William challenges. 'Whatever the rights and wrongs of the money, it still doesn't mean you didn't sexually harass Adelina. And it certainly doesn't mean you can break in here and threaten us.'

'Are you kidding?' David's voice rises with righteous indignation. 'Each and every one of those fifty thousand pounds is proof that something untoward happened and that you covered it up. I just don't know what that is, but you're going to tell me. And if you don't, then – well, not to be too much of a cliché, but I have ways of making you talk.'

David flashes the knife, the blade catching the light from the fitment above our heads. By this time in the evening, I'd have expected to have had the dinner plates cleared away and for my husband and me to be snuggled up together on the sofa with our favourite gritty crime drama on the TV. But I'm still surrounded by dirty dishes, and as for relaxing, I don't know if and when I'll ever be able to do that again.

But something else is happening here. For the first time since the three of us sat down, I'm sensing that my husband is becoming flustered. He's been surprisingly calm so far, as if he's become confident David won't actually hurt us if he hasn't done so already, and that he can talk his way out of this situation. But I tried that tactic myself with my offer of a pay-off – only for the announcement of an earlier pay-off, one that was news to me, to blow that idea spectacularly up in my face. But now that the fifty grand is out in the open, William seems less than assured, and he demonstrates his agitation by snapping at David again.

'I don't have to tell you anything!' he says angrily. 'This is my house. Mine. And I'll be damned if you can come in here and give me orders!'

'You seem to be forgetting who's wearing the handcuffs here,' David replies calmly. 'And you also seem to be forgetting that I can wait here all night for your children to return. What are their names? I probably asked you at work once, but I equally probably didn't listen to the answer. It would have just been me making polite conversation.'

'Well, you're certainly not being polite now,' William retorts.

'And you're certainly not making conversation,' David says. 'So how about you start trying a little harder and tell me what I need to know. You can tell your wife while we're at it, and make sure you tell her the truth this time. Tell us all about that secret payment to Adelina just before she left the company.' He tilts his nose and sniffs the air dramatically. 'Something is rotten here. It stinks. I can smell it. So what is it, William? What are you hiding?'

14

WILLIAM

Nights like this, my business card really goes to work.

It's a staff party, organised by me and funded by me, or at least it's funded by my expense account, one that I'm never shy in using because ultimately I'm the person who has the final sign-off on all the business accounts. Some people would argue that spending a load of money on food and drinks for staff might be a waste, but I see it as a necessary expense to keep morale high amongst my team.

And morale is certainly high this evening.

Twenty members of Gallagher's Ad Agency are crammed into this boutique bar in a trendy part of the city where we have spent all day completing a series of team-bonding exercises. I gave a short speech to start the day off, and then we spent the morning role-playing various sales scenarios in a meeting room at an upmarket hotel. The afternoon saw us running around an outdoor assault course, firing paintballs at each other. This is something I like to do once a year with half of the Gallagher staff, while Maria takes the other half for her version of team building at another time. We can't both be out of the office at the same time. Somebody has to keep the place on its toes.

Today, that hasn't been me.

My wife will be at home now winding down after what was likely another busy day, but I'm relaxing. Me and my colleagues are well fed after dinner at a fantastic Chinese restaurant just down the street from here, and now we're making sure that we're well watered, all thanks to my expense account.

I'm not going to lie. I love being in this position, and I don't just mean standing at the bar with colleagues beside me while I wait to order another round. I mean being the centre of attention. Being the one who has all the power. And make no mistake, whoever has the money has the power. Even from a very young age, I always noticed the influence money could have over people. My parents were wealthy, so my childhood is littered with memories of how that wealth could open doors for them. Those memories are perhaps what motivated me to work so hard, to build my own successful business and line the pockets of my bank accounts. I wanted not just the money, but all the power and status and finer things in life that come with it.

'Another bottle, please, there's a good man,' I call to the bartender when it's my turn to be served, and before I know it, I'm entering my credit card pin once again. It would be much easier if I could just set up a tab, but my finance manager had to persuade me that those weren't a good idea after last year when one such tab ended up totalling well over £5,000 after a couple of cheeky temps kept ordering the most expensive cocktails on the menu. Not realising what they were up to until the bill came meant that there was little we could do, but that was certainly a sobering night in the end. Needless to say, those temps were quickly dismissed when they failed to show for work the following day, but the bill still had to be paid, so now I keep things a little more under control.

But that doesn't mean I'm being cheap, far from it.

I spend the next fifteen minutes chatting about football with a couple of guys in the sales team. One of them, David, impresses me with his knowledge of the game, and I make a mental note to send him an invitation the next time I'm given free tickets to a local match. Another of the many perks of being in my position is that I often get sent freebies from companies pleased with the services we provide, so I'm sure it won't be long until I have some suitable tickets in my hand. But I also don't think it will be long until David has to call it a night here. He's swaying a little and has clearly been enjoying himself, not that I'll hold that against him.

To be honest, I'm not really the sort to hold a grudge. If I were, then I would already have a problem with David after he spent far too long flirting far too heavily with my wife at our last Christmas party. Maria kept her cool, while not encouraging him by any means, but there was almost a moment when I felt like I would have to step in and politely advise David to leave her alone. Thankfully, it hadn't come to that, so my and David's relationship remains cordial. But I know he has a roving eye when he's on a night out, which makes me wonder why he is here talking to me rather than on the other side of the bar, engaging some of our prettier colleagues in conversation.

'Tell me, David. How's the wedding planning going?' I ask, aware that he has a fiancée but intrigued as to whether or not he is genuinely committed to the woman he is set to exchange vows with.

'Meh, it's not really my thing,' David replies with a shrug that suggests it's not his idea of fun.

'Don't worry, once you're past this, you get to the real fun stuff. Married life. If you think things are boring now, wait until you get to that stage.'

I'm teasing him, but I am giving him some truth too. Now he looks worried, so I lighten the mood by reminding him that just because he has a partner, it doesn't mean he can't have a little fun.

'Why don't you go and talk to the ladies? The last time I checked, flirting is allowed in relationships.'

I gesture over to the group near the bar, but David just shrugs again.

'Yeah, maybe.'

'It's not like you to be shy.'

I give David a nudge that lets him know I remember some of his past exploits, and he looks a little sheepish as he most likely worries that I'm talking about his 'flirting' with Maria. But I don't mention that. Instead, I hand him a fresh beer and give him a gentle nudge.

'Go on. Have a chat. Socialise. Enjoy yourself,' I add as I send him on his way.

Alone for a moment, I take out my phone and see that I have a text message from Maria. She tells me that she has just managed to get Edward and Penny to settle down to sleep, and now she's thinking about an early night herself. It's half past ten, so I text her back, telling her that the day has been a success and that I'll be on my way back home soon enough.

As I put my phone away, I look up and see David chatting to Adelina, a colleague who has caught the eye of more than one man in the office since she started with us. She's strikingly good looking, for sure, but her softly spoken accent and direct way with words seem to make her irresistible to men. Whatever it is, she's got the wow factor, and David is certainly captivated. I watch as he says something to make her laugh before he puts his hand on her arm for a brief moment, a light touch but one that subtly lets her know they potentially could be closer than just two people who work together.

I let out a sigh as I watch the exchange, imagining what kind of mischief David could get up to tonight or indeed any night he wants, while I need to finish this drink and return to my homely duties. The kids will be up early in the morning. There will be hair to comb, schoolbags to find and breakfast to serve before they even set off on their way to school. And then I'll be faced with another full day of work.

So much responsibility. So many things to do.

Oh, to be young and free again.

Never mind, time to be sensible and do the grown-up thing here. And that means letting a few of my colleagues know that the free drinks have now come to an end. They're understandably disappointed, and while several of them thank me for the generous hospitality here this evening, they suggest they aren't ready for their 'team bonding' activities to be over yet.

They are going to move on to another bar.

They invite me too, but I tell them I'm going to call it a night, and as I finish my drink, I watch a handful of my employees drift out of the bar, emptying it significantly. But David and Adelina are still here, and I wonder how this night is going to play out for the two of them. David has his hand on her arm again, and he holds it there for longer this time, suggesting he is growing more comfortable with her and she in turn with him.

It's perhaps a little inappropriate given that I know he has a fiancée, but I can't help but think, *Good luck to you, David.*

But then I see him make a mistake. It's one that I sense he's probably made a lot in his life.

He suddenly becomes overconfident, most likely thanks

to his indulgence at the bar. The play he's making at Adelina becomes much more explicit, with none of the subtlety of before. He lurches in for a kiss.

But it's clear she isn't on the same wavelength as him.

I watch as she recoils, moving her head away and ensuring that his lips do not meet hers. He seems to apologise, or is it that he's annoyed? Whatever he says, it doesn't stop him from trying again, and this time Adelina leaves him completely, walking away towards the bar.

David looks very isolated all of a sudden, as well as more than a little foolish. He glances around, quickly downs his drink and heads for the door.

I guess he is right.

Life can be a bit 'meh', can't it?

I was on the verge of leaving myself, but after what I've just witnessed, I feel like I need to check Adelina is okay. I mean, it's not as if she was hurt or anything, and I'm sure it's not the first time she's rejected the advances of a man who's had too much to drink, but, as her boss, I should check she is okay.

'Hey, how's it going?' I ask as I position myself beside her at the bar.

'Oh, hey! I thought you'd left!'

'Almost. I just saw what happened – um, with you and David. Is everything okay?'

'Oh, that? Yeah, I'm fine. It was nothing. I think he just misread the signals.'

'And what signals were those?'

'Signals that say we're just friends.'

I laugh at that, then shrug, glad that there's nothing to it. Next thing, Adelina's getting the bartender's attention and ordering herself a wine before asking me if I want anything. She also lets me know that she's aware the free drinks have stopped now, but that she's happy to buy me one.

That's when I have the idea. The idea that all I have to do to make the free drinks flow again is take out my card and re-engage the powers of my company expense account. So that's what I do. I pick up the bill for Adelina's drink, and we enjoy a beverage together.

I also enjoy her company. She's funny, full of interesting stories about her life in Albania before she came here, and most interestingly of all, she is just the slightest bit flirtatious with me.

Maria and my children, as well as my work responsibilities, suddenly fade from my mind, and as the night wears on, I find myself being more and more enamoured with my colleague. So much so that I fail to realise just how late it is until the bartender tells us the bar is closing soon, and we're going to have to finish our drinks and leave.

It's after midnight when I stagger out into the street with Adelina beside me, the two of us laughing at a joke I've just made about a difficult client we both know. Then she looks around for a taxi, and I should probably do the same.

But I'm only looking at her.

Her eyes. Her lips. Her beauty.

And then, just like David, I lean forward to kiss her.

'Hey, what are you doing?' Adelina says, and she puts her hand on my chest to prevent me getting any closer. But it doesn't really work because I'm bigger and stronger than her, so I try again, and this time our lips actually meet.

'William! Stop!' she cries, looking at me aghast.

'What's wrong? You like me, don't you?'

'Like is not the point. You're married!'

'Don't worry about that. Come here.'

I try again for that kiss, and as Adelina backs up, she bumps into the wall behind her. She has nowhere to go, and as I press myself up against her, I understand that this is the true benefit of being the boss. Forget the expense account;

this is way more fun than that. This is real power. And it's a power that means I can fully expect my employee to comply with what I want.

Adelina wriggles as I kiss her, and I start to move my hands over her body. She tries to push me off again, but I don't budge, and as my hands keep moving, I'm waiting for that moment when she will relent and gasp that this is what she wanted all along.

But it doesn't happen. Instead, her knee hits my groin, and all the oxygen gets sucked out of me. I pull back and see nothing but anger on Adelina's face.

She takes her chance to escape, and while I want to go after her, I'm still too sore and too winded to make any sudden movements. That's why I can't catch her before she disappears around the corner, and by the time I do start running, she is being driven away in the back of a taxi.

'Damn it,' I say as I stand alone on the dark city street. 'What have I done?'

15

THE MORNING AFTER

WILLIAM

I haven't slept. Having arrived home in the early hours and crawled into bed beside my sleepy wife, I mumbled an apology for staying out later than planned, blamed it on a couple of colleagues who persuaded me to have 'one more drink', and then let her get some rest. But there was no rest for me. I've spent hours tossing and turning in the bed, replaying the events on the street outside that bar in my head, but even as dawn breaks and sunlight seeps in around the curtains, I have not been able to retell this story in any way that this is not a complete disaster for me.

Adelina ran away from me after I forced myself on her. Is she okay? Did she go home? Did she go to the police? Am I going to be arrested for what happened? Is my wife going to find out that I'm not as perfect as she thinks I am? And what about my children? What are they going to hear? That their daddy is a horrible man, a man who treats women like objects?

Is that what I am?

The silence in this house is excruciating and is only making my troubled mind feel more and more jangled. So I peel back the duvet and tiptoe out of bed, leaving Maria lost in the bliss of whatever dreamlike state she is in while I endure this torturous hell of wondering what Adelina might do next.

Whichever way I spin it, she has the power to destroy my life.

I make my way to the bathroom, have a shave and try to stay positive. What if she doesn't see it as such a big deal? What if she puts it down to the fact that I had too much to drink and excuses it? What if she forgives me? I am her boss, after all, so maybe she'll decide it's in her best interests not to cause trouble.

The more I force myself to think along these lines, the more I convince myself everything might just be okay. But, in reality, I know that I'm never really going to know the truth until I go into the office and face the music. I cringe at the thought, but if Adelina is there, then perhaps I can make a swift apology, and that can be the end of it. But if she isn't? Then I'll still have no idea how she's taken what happened – and the nerves will really kick in.

I need to get out of the house and into the office as quickly as possible, so I get dressed and grab my briefcase, all while trying not to wake Maria. But she stirs just before I can slip out of the room, and when she sees me in my suit standing by the doorway, she asks what I am doing.

'I couldn't sleep, so I'm going to go in early and get a head start on the day,' I tell her. 'Will you be okay to get the kids ready?'

'Er, yeah, sure. Has something happened?'

'What? No, everything's fine. You know I never sleep particularly well after a few drinks the night before.'

'A few drinks? You were out until one o'clock.'

'Err, yeah. It was silly of me. But I'm not feeling too bad now. I'll grab a coffee on the way to the office, and I'll be fine.'

Maria doesn't look sure, but I do my best to smile even though I'm a mess on the inside, and she eventually smiles back at me before returning to her pillow.

I grimace when I think about what precarious position my wife might find me in at our workplace when she does report for duty later this morning, but I'm hoping I'll have been able to put out this 'fire' before then, and with a bit of luck, she'll never know what I did with one of our employees while she was dutifully at home looking after our children.

The roads are quiet at this early hour, so despite driving cautiously, as I sense there might still be alcohol sloshing around my system, I make it into the office in record time.

I use my pass to access the building and wave to the security guard who has been here on duty all night before asking if anybody else is already in.

'Just Becky,' he replies, and while I'm pleased that Adelina hasn't rushed into the office so soon, the fact that the HR manager is here might not be particularly good news. If Adelina does make a complaint against me, then it's Becky who will see it first. That's why I decide to go and see her before I reach my own office. I knock on her door and hear her voice inviting me in a moment later.

'Good morning,' I say, entering with confidence, keen not to appear like a condemned man just yet.

'Oh, hey! You're in early,' Becky replies with one hand on her keyboard and the other on a half-eaten bacon sandwich that she instantly looks guilty about.

'I could say the same about you. I'd have asked you to

bring me a sarnie too if I'd known. Brown sauce, please.' I smile lamely at my own joke. 'Is everything okay?'

'Yeah, it's fine. I didn't sleep too well, so thought I'd come in and get an early start before the tiredness overwhelms me later.'

'I see. Same here.'

'That wouldn't have anything to do with the team drinks, would it?' Becky asks, and I freeze in fear that she already knows far more than she is letting on.

'The drinks? What do you mean?'

'You had the bonding day with the sales team yesterday, right? I'm sure that didn't end early.'

Becky gives me a wink then, and I feel a bit awkward, but it also allows me to relax because she really wouldn't have done that if she knew what had happened.

'Oh, right. The team-bonding day. Yeah, it was fun. Not much to report.'

'Is that the truth, or are you just saying that because I'm the HR manager?'

My heart rate spikes dramatically, then plummets as Becky laughs and winks again.

Relax, William. She's just teasing you.

Confident that nothing has been reported to her yet, I'm just about to leave her office when she oh-so-casually mentions something that is big, big news for me.

'Do you know if anything happened with Adelina yesterday?'

'What?'

'It's just that she emailed me an hour ago asking if she could meet to discuss something that took place yesterday. And I'm afraid it doesn't sound good.'

'Oh dear.' I try to compose myself. 'What did she say?'

'That she was harassed by a male member of staff.'

Oh God. She's going to report me. There's going to be an inves-

tigation. I'm going to lose my place in my company. And then I'll lose my wife and kids.

'What?'

'Yeah, I was shocked too. Do you have any idea what might have happened?'

'No, none at all,' I reply, hoping that I'm as convincing a liar as I need to be to get out of this awkward exchange.

'Okay, well, I'll see what she has to say when she comes to see me.'

'Do you know what time that'll be?'

'I'm not sure. She didn't say. But she must have been awake early to send me that email, so I'm guessing she won't be too long.'

'Right. No problem. Yeah, just let me know the score once you've spoken to her.'

'Will do. And I'll obviously have to inform the other members of the management team about the allegation as well.'

'Will you?'

'Yes.' She gives me an odd look. 'That's the rules.'

Shit. She's right.

Our company policy, the one I set out with Maria when we first started our business, is that any serious allegations that involve members of staff must be discussed openly amongst the management team. That way everybody can be kept in the loop, and there can be less chance of us being accused of a cover-up, which could happen if only one or two people were privy to the information.

'Of course. Fine,' I reply, trying to sound authoritative, but aware that it is as far from fine as it is possible to get.

Becky eyes her bacon sandwich then, clearly ready for me to leave her office so she can get back to it, but she doesn't need to worry about me lingering for too long now. I have no intention of staying up here on the sixth floor. Instead, I'm immediately on my way down to the ground floor, where I can wait for Adelina to arrive in reception. That way I can intercept her before she makes it to Becky's office. Doing so is my only chance of preventing a disaster.

Descending to the ground floor, I feel my stomach lurching like I'm travelling at 100 mph and not the gentle pace the lift operates at. By the time the doors slide open, I feel like I could be sick all over the polished marble floor of the reception area, but I manage to keep myself composed as I pass the security guard again and go outside. Then I nervously scan the vehicles in the car park, looking for any sign of Adelina. I'm sure her arrival is imminent, and she'll probably want to get inside before she thinks I'm here. But I'm already on-site, and that means I am ready when I see her arriving ten minutes later.

I wait until she is out of her car before I approach her, but she does not react well when she sees me.

'What are you doing?' she cries as I reach her, and it's obvious that the last time we were together has made her anxious still in my presence.

'I need to talk to you about last night.'

'I have nothing to say to you.'

'But I have something to say to you. I want to apologise for what happened. It was a terrible mistake. I honestly didn't mean to upset you.'

'You didn't mean to upset me? You forced yourself on me. You wouldn't get off me. I thought you were going to …'

Adelina doesn't finish her sentence, but she doesn't need to. I know full well what her next words would be.

'No, no. Please. That wasn't going to happen. It was just a kiss, and I regret it. I'm sorry.' I shift my tone a little. 'I hope you understand that it doesn't have to go any further.'

'You don't get to make that decision for me,' she declares, and she goes to walk past me. I know she will go straight into the office and tell Becky everything. So for the second time in twenty-four hours, I try to stop Adelina from doing what she wants to.

'Wait! Please don't do this. Don't report me.'

'How do you know that's what I'm going to do?'

I'm not sure I should tell her what I say next, but it feels like I have no option. 'I saw Becky this morning. She said you had made an allegation, but I know you haven't said who it's against. Adelina, it's not too late to stop.'

'And why would I stop?'

Adelina eyeballs me, and it's very clear that a change of tactics is needed if I'm to get her to come around to my way of thinking. Persuading with just words isn't going to work. I need something else. Something more tangible, something more powerful.

'I'll give you money,' I say instinctively.

'What?' She looks a little shocked, but the curious lift of her eyebrows makes me hopeful.

'I'll pay you not to say anything. Please.'

'Really?' Her expression has turned steely. 'How much?'

I hadn't thought about it, but I need to come up with a number quick.

'Ten grand.'

She thinks about it for a moment before shaking her head.

'Not interested.'

Then Adelina tilts her chin as if our conversation is over, and goes to walk past me.

'Twenty!' I almost shout in desperation, wanting to resolve this before more people arrive here.

That gets her attention.

'You're serious?'

'Yes, I am.'

'Then that just proves how much you know what you did

was wrong. So thank you for the not-so-generous offer, but I'd rather let everybody know what kind of man you really are. I think I'll start with your wife, see what she has to say.'

'Thirty!'

I'm at the point where I'd almost say any number now just to get Adelina to stop.

She pauses, as if considering her options, so I double down on my offer.

'Thirty grand. In your account this week. All you have to do is cancel that meeting with Becky.'

'And then what? We go back to working together as if we're best friends?'

'I didn't say that. Maybe you might think about moving on at some point. I'd give you an excellent reference of course. Make sure you find an even better job than the one you have now.'

'Wow. You are desperate to buy my silence, aren't you?'

It's pathetic, but Adelina can see just how weak I am. She holds my fate in her hands.

So, what will she do?

She accepts my offer.

Relief washes over me, and I have to stop myself reaching to shake her hand as if we'd just concluded a business deal. Instead, as we go into the office, we iron out the details again. And Adelina does what I need her to. She goes to Becky and apologises for a misunderstanding and says she isn't pressing ahead with any allegation now.

That should be it. The end. Except it's not because Becky calls me an hour later to say she can't just drop the matter because something obviously happened that's made Adelina too scared to confront the situation – and her alleged harasser.

I try to say that Adelina is perfectly within her rights, but Becky isn't having it. She says an allegation like that has to be thoroughly investigated because there's 'no smoke without fire', and if there is a culture issue at the company, then it needs to be laid bare so it can be rectified. She then mentions that she has already emailed the other managers to let them know such an allegation has been made.

I'd normally be thrilled that I had a HR manager who was so passionate about making sure that precisely the right thing was done, but not in this case. I know I'm going to have to return to Adelina with another proposition. The allegation of sexual harassment has to be pinned to somebody before Becky questions Adelina and Adelina crumbles and tells the truth. So we need another name. Somebody who could take the fall for this. Another guy in the office who people could believe was capable of sexual harassment.

Someone who would have no choice but to take whatever punishment the managers decide on.

Anyone. Anyone but me.

So I suggest David to Adelina. He's got a reputation for trying it on with women at staff parties, and that should be enough to convince other people of his guilt. But Adelina refuses to pin my crime on somebody else.

I have to up my offer.

I have to go all the way up to a new number.

£50,000.

That's what it will take to keep me out of trouble.

That's what it will take to change David's life for ever.

16

DAVID

I'm frustrated. This day and night have already gone on far longer than they should have, and I'm tired of listening to William and Maria continue to protest their innocence. I'm also getting more and more angry at William because he is still trying to make out like the £50,000 payment he made to Adelina was no big deal.

'I swear it was just to keep her from telling anybody that she had been harassed in our workplace,' William says again. 'My wife and I have worked too hard to build up our business to see its reputation ruined by the actions of an employee who couldn't keep his lecherous hands to himself.'

William has real venom in his voice, and I can see that he's convinced himself of my guilt, presumably because that way, he can justify all of this. But I know that he had no evidence, so why was he so eager to take Adelina's word for it?

And why fling so much money at her before she left the company?

'This isn't working,' I decide as I stand up, the knife in my hand and a new plan starting to form in my mind. And it's a plan that doesn't end well for the couple in handcuffs.

'I want justice, but it seems the only way I'll get it now is by taking matters into my own hands,' I say, and I walk around behind the pair, making each of them extremely uncomfortable as they wriggle and turn their heads to see what I will do next.

'Please don't hurt us,' Maria begs. 'There has to be another way we can sort this out. There has to be a way we can find Adelina, and then we can all talk about this together. What do you think?'

'I've told you already! Adelina is gone!' I cry at a volume that causes the couple to flinch. But that's not all I am going to do to them, and as I put the knife to Maria's neck again, I am fully prepared to end this with bloodshed. Rather that than allow this couple to carry on living a life of luxurious bliss while I rot in a life of torture that I didn't choose for myself.

'She hasn't gone!' William shouts before the blade can do any damage to Maria's vulnerable neck.

'What?'

I pause, my hand shaking slightly as I grip the knife's handle.

'Adelina. She hasn't gone. She's still in the UK. She's still close.'

'You know where she is?' I'm staggered at this turn of events, but suspicious too, aware that he might simply be trying to trick me.

'Yes, I do! And I can take you to her. I'll take you there right now. Just don't hurt my wife, please.'

This is not a development that I expected, but the opportunity to speak to Adelina and find out why she buried me under the crushing weight of a false allegation is one that I can't pass on.

'So. Where is she?' I ask as I increase the distance between the knife and the trembling Maria's neck.

'She lives in a house across town,' William replies. 'Sharples Road.'

'How do you know?'

'Because I have kept tabs on her after she left the company. I wanted to make sure that she didn't go back on her word about not telling anyone about the allegation or the pay-off.'

'You kept tabs on her?' I repeat, trying to understand this. 'Have you been sleeping with her?'

'What? No, of course not! I swear!' William cries. 'I just got her new address as part of our deal for her not to speak to the media. I said if she had no intention of breaking her word, then she wouldn't have to worry. And she hasn't. Everything has been fine.'

'So she's at this address right now?' I ask, my hopes rising now that there might be a way for me to finally get the truth from my accuser. Or at least I'll know where she is.

So I can kill her for ruining my life.

One or the other.

'Yes, she lives there,' William replies. 'And she's probably home. So I can take you there. Then we can sort this out, and you'll see that neither me nor my wife have done anything wrong. Then you can leave us alone after that. Right?'

'I will decide what happens after that,' I say sternly. 'Okay, let's go and pay Adelina a visit. Both of you up, now.'

I give the couple a nudge to get them to rise out of their seats, and they do as they're told, but William isn't happy.

'No, I'll take you,' he insists, 'but Maria stays here. That's the condition.'

'You're in no position to be making demands,' I reply without skipping a beat. 'We all go together. We'll take your car. Come on. Get moving.'

I usher the handcuffed couple out of the dining room and in the direction of the front door, swiping the car key from the bowl on the hallway table.

'I've always wanted to drive a car like yours,' I say as I inspect the insignia on the key fob. 'At least something good has come out of all this.'

'Please just let my wife stay here,' William tries again but to no avail. I push them both out of the front door and towards the luxury vehicle parked on the driveway.

I unlock it with the push of a button, and the doors open. I tell William and Maria to get onto the back seat. William again tries to persuade me to just take him, but Maria actually seems happy enough to go along, and she clambers in first. Perhaps she's eager for confirmation that her husband has definitely not been sleeping with Adelina like I just suggested.

William reluctantly gets into the car before I take my seat behind the wheel and start the engine. I am ready to go.

'Okay, you can direct me,' I say to William, catching his eyes in the rear-view mirror. 'And try to relax, you two. Don't look so worried. Forget about the cuffs. We're just going for a nice drive.'

With that, I put my foot down on the accelerator and hear the satisfying roar of the engine. Then I set off, pulling out onto the quiet road that leads up to the big house that very nearly became a bloody and shocking murder scene.

17

MARIA

I might hate the man currently behind the wheel, but I have to give him credit for one thing. He drives this car a lot more sensibly than my husband does.

I wasn't thrilled when William told me that he was treating himself to a so-called supercar, not because I have a problem with him rewarding himself with an extravagant gift but because I have a rough idea of the top speeds vehicles like this one can achieve. I wasn't exactly excited about the thought of him speeding through the country lanes near our house, particularly if he took the kids out for a drive too.

While he's always assured me that he would never do anything to put our children at risk, I know he takes a fair few risks when it's just him in the car; my husband likes to joke he has petrol running through his veins – he feels the need for speed. Thankfully, he's never crashed or even come close as far as I'm aware, but that doesn't mean I haven't always felt relieved when he's opted for one of our less powerful vehicles to get him to his destination.

But there is no danger of us crashing this evening, because David is driving very cautiously, clearly having underestimated how difficult it might be to drive an unfamiliar car in the dark with the additional stress of transporting two handcuffed passengers.

I haven't seen any other cars since we left our house and started heading through these lanes, but I'm hoping that will change. I really want to try to shout for help from any passing drivers. I don't know if they will hear me or see that my wrists are restrained when I hold them up to the window, but I'm definitely going to give it my best shot. I know it'll make David angry if he sees me, but I'm counting on there being not much he can do about it from the driver's seat. If he wants to punish me, he'll have to pull over, but stopping the car to threaten me with the knife might give any other motorist more of a chance to realise something is wrong and call the police, which I'd obviously welcome. But all this remains conjecture: our headlights are still the only ones cutting through the darkness.

As for the silence, there are only two things cutting through that. One of them is the low hum of the car engine. The other is my husband's voice as he directs David to Adelina's house.

Adelina's house.

While I'm in complete shock about the fact that William gave her a secret £50,000 pay-off, I'm just as shocked that he knows where she now lives. Like most people at our company, and like David, I had been under the impression that Adelina had returned to her native Albania after she left us. But apparently not. And not only is she apparently still local, my husband knows her exact address.

Why? He said it was so he could make sure she didn't reveal details of the sexual harassment incident. But is that really likely? Or has something been going on between them, something more than all the secrets they already seem to have?

I've always been aware that my husband is not perfect, he's human after all; I've never worried about him being unfaithful. He's never given me any reason to suspect him of cheating, which is the way it should be in a marriage, but I know life isn't that simple. Things happen. But now I do suspect him. And I suspect him with a very particular woman. An attractive, charismatic and smart woman, one who was his employee. He certainly had the opportunity to get close to her if that was what he wanted.

But did he? Has he been having sex with her, then coming home to me? Or is he telling the truth that this is all still part of the harassment claim, the one that David seems willing to kill over, so vehement is his denial of his guilt?

Like the man driving this car, I'm hoping for some serious answers when we get to Adelina's place, unless, of course, I can find a way to escape before we get there.

'Take a left here,' William says, and David steers us around another corner, but, alas, there are no other head-lights on this road either.

I stare out of the window beside me at the dark fields passing us by, fields that I usually find so pretty when I drive by them in daylight. This really is a beautiful part of the country, and I always felt like I was lucky to call it home. But now I'm rather wishing we had moved to the middle of a big, noisy, sprawling city. It would be so much harder to be kidnapped there, which is essentially what is happening to us here.

Another few corners are rounded before we make it onto a main road with houses dotted on either side. But all the

lights are off, and nobody is up and looking out of their property to spot us going past. If only the people sleeping in their
beds knew that a major crime was taking place right under
their noses. As it is, they'll maybe never know, or perhaps
they will only find out when they read the morning headlines
when drinking their first coffee of the day.

Terror hits our town!

Local couple held at knifepoint by a dangerous intruder!

*Meet the Gallaghers – lovers, business owners and now
murder victims ...*

Just some of the headlines journalists might choose,
although I sincerely hope that last one is just my imagination
running away with me. But as we turn another corner, I sigh
with the realisation that only the man steering this car knows
what is going to happen next.

And then I see them.

The pair of headlights up ahead, two bluish-white glows
in the darkness.

And they're coming straight towards us.

This is my chance.

I waste no time in pressing my face against the window
and holding my handcuffed arms up so they are fully on
show when the car passes us.

*And then I start screaming for help. Really screaming with
every bit of breath in my body.*

I feel the car wobble slightly and assume that I have startled David with my sudden loud noises. But I don't care. I
only care that the driver of the other car sees and hears me
because if they do, then they will surely call the police and
tell them that a woman is being held against her will. They

will be able to describe the car, and I doubt there are too many vehicles like this one cruising around at this time of night, so the police should have no trouble tracking us down quickly, thus ending David's reign of terror and ensuring I get to see my children in the morning. Then the dust can settle on this horrible, frightening nightmare.

'Shut up!' David yells, but why should I listen to him now?

I carry on shouting, frantic to attract attention as the headlights get closer, and then I go even further, banging my hands and my head against the window in sheer desperation.

'Shut your wife up now, or I'll do it for you!' David shouts over me, but William doesn't come to his aid. He just starts shouting too, and while he's on the opposite side to the car that is about to pass us, he's making as much noise and being as visible as he can to increase our chance of being discovered.

David is furious, and the car veers alarmingly on the road, stacking up the odds that this other driver will suspect something untoward. But then they pass us, and despite there being two handcuffed, screaming passengers in a car that surely anyone would take a closer look at, the driver doesn't even so much as turn his head as he goes past.

But I catch sight of him: an elderly man in his eighties who looks like he is doing all he can to see over his own steering wheel, never mind pay attention to somebody else's, and as he rolls on into the night, our chance at escape seems to go with him.

'No! Come back!' I cry, but it's no good. The car has gone. *And now David is slowing down.*

'What are you doing?' William asks as he parks up at the roadside, but David doesn't answer. He just gets out of the car and comes around to the back. Then he opens the door beside me and drags me out onto the road.

'No! Get off me!' I cry before David puts a hand over my mouth to silence me. Then he heaves me towards the back of the car, opens the trunk and tries to bundle me inside.

My screams are muffled against his palm as I do my best to resist, but he's considerably stronger than me, and despite doing everything I can to resist him, he's somehow able to shove me in and bring the door down shut hard on me.

And then everything goes dark.

I'm trapped now. I feel myself begin to panic. Not only is it terrifying to be in such total darkness, but I've never been a big fan of enclosed spaces. Even at work, I usually avoid the lift if I can help it, as well as the tiny cupboard where we keep the stationery. Claustrophobia. Which means this is one of the worst possible places where I could find myself.

Why didn't I just stay quiet? Why did I have to cause trouble? If only I hadn't screamed, then David would have just left me where I was. Now I'm locked in here, and who knows when I'll be coming out again.

I really start screaming. I beg to be let out. I beg for oxygen. I beg for my life.

But all that happens is that I hear the engine get louder, and I feel the car move again.

It seems he's going to drive the rest of the way to Adelina's house with me in the trunk of the car.

I stop screaming when I realise no one can possibly hear me. I realise, too, that it might be best to try to save some air because there must be a limited amount in here. But that thought only causes me to start hyperventilating, and now I really feel overwhelmed by anxiety because I can sense I'm on the verge of a panic attack, and that's the last thing I need.

It takes all my strength to keep myself from having a total breakdown, but I manage it, and despite the tears and sweat pouring down my face, I am able to return my breathing to a steadier level.

I have no idea how much time has passed before I feel the car come to a stop. When I do, I hear the engine rumble off, followed by the sound of a door opening and closing.

Is this it? Are we here?

Are we at Adelina's house?

18

DAVID

I hadn't planned on locking Maria in the trunk of a car tonight, but then again, I hadn't planned any of this six months ago. *Unpredictable.* That's how my life has been over this past half a year, so I'm not going to worry too much about dealing with whatever residual trauma might be left over from all these actions of mine when tonight is over. I am just staying focused on the task at hand, and right now, that is going into the house I'm parked outside and getting the woman inside to explain why she lied about me.

Peering out at the house I've been instructed to stop at, I see closed curtains across the windows and a distinct lack of light or activity. It might appear that nobody is home, but at this time of night, the person within is most likely sleeping. But I want a little more confirmation that I am in the right place before I knock on the front door.

'This is it? Adelina's here?' I ask William, and he nods.

'Yeah, this is it.'

'The place looks empty.'

'It's the middle of the night. She'll be in bed.'

'Then I guess I'd better wake her up. But before I do that ...'

I turn and reach into the back of the car then and grab William's handcuffed wrists before instructing the man to sit forward. William struggles a little, but I work fast, unlocking the handcuffs quickly before wrapping them around the steering wheel, ensuring William is now very much stuck in place in this car.

'I wouldn't want you to think about trying to make a run for it while I'm in the house,' I say as William wriggles his wrists and tries to free himself. But it only confirms that he is now locked to the steering wheel, and with his wife locked in the trunk, I know that my two prisoners aren't going anywhere until I return.

'Okay, I'm off to wake up Sleeping Beauty,' I say as I get out of the car while ignoring William's protests.

Closing the door on him, all is quiet out on this residential street. But then I hear something else. It's muffled and very faint, but I can hear it nonetheless.

It's the sound of Maria begging for help.

I walk around and rest my hand on the glossy metal lid that's keeping Maria trapped. But I have no intention of opening it up and letting her out. One thing is for sure. She is certainly quieter in there than she would be out here.

Turning my attention back to the dark house, I walk up the narrow pathway that leads to the front door before taking a deep breath and knocking three times. I don't knock so loudly as to wake any of the neighbours, but it's hopefully loud enough to wake anybody who might be sleeping in this property. That's why it feels strange when nobody comes to answer the door.

So I knock again. And again. But still nobody comes. Not even a single light has been turned on inside, and that is very strange. Adelina supposedly lives here, so why isn't she answering? She can't know who it is trying to get her to come to the door, so that can't be the problem. I wonder if Adelina is staying elsewhere tonight. Or perhaps it's that Adelina doesn't like answering the door at this time of night, which would make sense as a woman living alone. Or maybe there is another reason why she isn't answering the door.

Maybe it's because she isn't here at all.

Maybe William has been toying with me.

Maybe William has been deliberately stalling.

As I turn back to the car, I see the shape of William leaning into the front seat, his hands still on the wheel while his eyes are just visible inside the dark vehicle as they stare out at me.

I decide to spend a little more time looking around before going back to demand some answers from William, so I try to look in a few of the windows, although that shows me nothing but curtains. Then I make my way down the side of the house, kicking open a wooden gate into a back garden that is very small and very minimalist. It doesn't look like Adelina is much of a gardener if the long grass and mass of unsightly weeds along the back fence are anything to go by. But this garden's unkempt state could be a symptom of something else beyond a lack of outdoor endeavour. It could be a sign that nobody has lived at this property for a while, and if that is the case, William really is wasting my time here.

Trying the back door but finding it locked, I throw a couple of small stones at the upstairs windows to see if that stirs anybody inside. Getting no response, I give up and return to the front of the house.

Convinced that there is nobody inside, I go back to question William, but when I do, I find him full of excuses.

'She'll definitely be in there. You can't have been loud enough. I get it, you don't want to make too much noise on this street. I'll help you. I'll wake her up. She's definitely in there.'

I think about letting William out to assist me, but that seems risky, and there is nothing to indicate that he'd fare any better than I managed myself. That's why I tell him that I'm not letting him out. I feel like I am being played somewhere here. I no longer trust that William is genuinely trying to help me see Adelina. With that in mind, it is time for the knife to make an appearance again.

But the re-emergence of the blade acts as the catalyst for William saying something that surprises me, and it would certainly have surprised Maria as well, if only she hadn't been locked in the trunk.

'Look, I swear she is in there. She's just a very deep sleeper.'

'Oh, right. And how do you know that?'

'I just know.'

'How?'

'Think about it.'

'I don't have time for this. Tell me.'

'Because … I've slept with her.'

I laugh out loud at that. I can't help but find it deeply amusing that this man, with his once seemingly perfect life, is now being threatened at knifepoint while handcuffed to the wheel of his own car as he confesses to cheating on his wife. Who, by the way, is locked in the trunk of the very same car.

Forget my life being unpredictable. William's might be even crazier.

'You've slept with Adelina?' I say, trying to make sense of this.

'Ssssh! Keep your voice down. Please!' William replies.

Despite everything, he's clearly nervous about his wife over-hearing us.

'So what? You've been having an affair with her? Is that it?'

'I wouldn't call it an affair.'

'What would you call it? Or, more importantly perhaps, what would your wife call it?'

'It's nothing, just something that happened a couple of times. It was a stupid mistake, and I regret it.'

'So that's how you know where she lives? You've been here before? You've slept with her here?'

William doesn't answer that, so I take it as a yes.

'Look, I'm not proud of it,' William says quietly, and to be fair to him, he does look broken in that moment. Then again, it is easy for anybody in his position to look broken, so I'm not going to give him too much sympathy. Rather, I want to know if this affair has anything to do with what happened to me.

'Is this why you believed Adelina when she made the false claim against me? Why you were so quick to take her side? Because she was your lover? Is it why you gave her all that money too?'

'Look, it's not as black and white as that.'

'Isn't it? It seems pretty clear to me. You had a mistress, a very attractive mistress, and she was able to get you to do whatever she wanted. She told you to fire me, didn't she? And she asked you for money, which you gave her? Admit it, you're just another rich guy who's been taken advantage of by a hot young woman.'

'No, that's not it.'

'Then what is it, then?'

'I genuinely thought you had harassed her. And I paid her to keep quiet so the company name wasn't dragged through the mud.'

'You expect me to believe that after what you've just told me?'

'Yes, because it's the truth!'

William raised his voice then, probably unintentionally, and I gesture towards the back of the car to remind him that he might not want to do that again.

'Careful, you don't want your wife hearing this conversation. Remember?'

That shuts William up, allowing me a moment to think. I guess there is still a chance that he is telling the truth, however unlikely. If Adelina did have some kind of vendetta against me, whatever that might have been, it's just about plausible that she might have made up a lie and convinced William to believe it. But the only way to start to piece this puzzle together is to speak to the woman in question, and that still seems impossible if we can't get her to answer the door.

'Let me come with you,' William says, his voice quiet but urgent. 'I'll get her to answer the door, I swear.'

I think about it but not for long because I only have two options. Say no and leave William in the car but not speak to Adelina tonight. Or say yes and potentially get a resolution to all of this – if William is being honest about how he can get Adelina out of bed to face us.

'Okay, I'll let you try. But I swear to God, if you are tricking me, I will kill you right here and lay your body out on the back seat. Then I'll drive this car into the nearest lake with your wife still trapped in the trunk. Do you understand me?'

William nods quickly, his face afraid and compliant. Only then do I remove the handcuffs from around the steering wheel so William can get out of the car, still handcuffed but at least able to move around more freely again. As I pull him away from the car towards the house, I accidentally drop the key to the handcuffs and am unable to find it again in the dark. But it's hardly my biggest problem right now, so I move on.

I lead William to the front door, intrigued to see what my prisoner might do differently to rouse Adelina.

'Around the back,' William says.

'I've already tried that.'

'Let's try again.'

I'm willing to give it one more go, so I march William down the side of the house, one hand on his shoulder and the other on the knife that I'm keeping raised, ready to strike if needed.

Once we are in the garden, I tell William how I already tried the back door before mentioning the stones I threw at the windows.

'Which one is her bedroom?' I ask.

'That one,' William replies, nodding towards the upstairs window on the left.

'Tell me, did you ever feel guilty when you were up there having sex with somebody who wasn't your wife?' I ask, taunting my prisoner slightly, but William doesn't take the bait. Instead, he just wanders down the overgrown path that leads to the back fence.

What are you doing?' I call after him, but William ignores me and keeps moving along, nudging various bits of rockery as he goes. And that's when we both hear it. It's the sound of something metallic clinking across the concrete of the path. We both look down to see what has just fallen out from underneath one of the disturbed rocks.

It's a key.

'She'd mentioned a spare key,' William says as he crouches down to try to pick it up.

'I'll get it,' I say, swiping it up before William has the chance.

I inspect the key in my hand before asking William why he didn't tell me about it sooner.

'I didn't know exactly where it was,' he tries, but I cut him off, telling him I don't believe him. That's when William admits he kept it quiet so he could get out of the car.

But why?

'I want to speak to Adelina too,' he tells me. 'I want to get the truth just as much as you do. I have a feeling she has screwed both of us here, not just you.'

I roll my eyes at that because I'm hardly sympathetic to his plight over mine. Then I walk to the back door and insert the key into the lock. When I turn it, I am pleased to hear a soft click, indicating that it is now open.

'I guess we're going in, then,' I say before I usher William over to me and tell him that we will go in together, William first, and me behind, the knife ready if I should need to use it on either my prisoner or Adelina.

Entering the quiet home, I locate the nearest light switch, and suddenly, we are standing in a small kitchen, bathed in light. It's clean and sparse. Nothing like the wild garden we've just left.

'Is she always this tidy?' I ask, but William just shrugs and looks towards the next doorway.

Moving through it, another flick of a light switch reveals a cosy living room with a neat sofa and a compact TV as well as a rug in front of a fireplace that looks like it might not have been used for a while.

'She is very minimalist, isn't she?' I say as I look around. 'She certainly hasn't spent much of that fifty grand on furniture for this place.'

But William remains silent, just looks towards the staircase ahead of us.

I consider calling up to Adelina and making our presence

known so she can come down and meet us, but I decide it would be better to keep the element of surprise and startle the woman in her bedroom. One good thing, I realise, from all my failed efforts to rouse her is that she must surely be alone in the house.

'Come on, let's go up,' I say, pushing William towards the stairs. 'And be quiet.'

We begin to ascend, our feet moving softly over the carpeted steps until we make it to the landing, where we are faced with three dark doorways.

'Which one is her bedroom?' I ask, and William nods towards the third doorway.

'Well, I'm sure you had a lot more fun the last time you were in there than you're going to have tonight,' I snap as I push William towards the bedroom while raising my knife a little higher. I really want Adelina to get a good look at the weapon when we enter.

But while there is a bed in here, there is nobody sleeping in it.

No one to panic when she sees two men entering.

No one to scream when she sees the knife and realises the man she set up has come back to seek his revenge.

No Adelina.

It's at that point that I'm suddenly knocked off balance as William uses his shoulder to barge into me, causing the knife to fall to the floor before I can do anything about it. Then I feel a blinding pain in my skull and nose as I realise that William has headbutted me. I stagger back out of the bedroom to try to put some space between me and my handcuffed attacker. But William surges forward again, driving his entire bodyweight into me, and I feel myself succumbing to sheer gravity.

I fall backwards and grab at thin air, but there is nothing to halt my momentum now, and I tumble all the way down the stairs, hitting my head and jarring every bone in my body as I go.

In an agonised, dazed heap at the bottom of the stairs, I know I have to try to get to my feet before William comes down and attacks me while I am in this vulnerable position. It is obvious now that he has tricked me into coming here, but all I care about at this moment is surviving this so I can live another day to make a new plan.

But William doesn't give me that chance.

He charges down the stairs, and once at the bottom, he begins kicking my body before stamping on my head, and while I beg for mercy, there is none.

William doesn't stop until I feel like I'm inches from death. He must sense it too because it's only then that he pauses for breath and takes a look around this house that is just about to bear witness to a grisly murder.

My own breath is becoming ever more of a struggle, the pain excruciating, my lungs and heart beyond repair. Yet somehow it strikes me as horribly absurd that my dying thoughts should be of this murderer and the property we're in. I realise it must belong to him, not to that vivacious woman I once made a fool of myself with …

19

WILLIAM

The estate agent's name is Miranda, and I waste no time in checking out her impressive curves whenever she turns her back to me. I've certainly stolen plenty of sneaky glances during this thirty-minute appointment as she shows me around this small but suitable property that I am considering putting an offer in for.

'Here's the master bedroom,' Miranda says as she leads me into a room with a double bed, nightstand and a wardrobe in the corner.

It's not the biggest room, but none of the rooms in this house are big. But there's a charm about its size, and while it's much smaller than the house I share with my wife, I don't need this one to be big.

I just need it to stay a secret.

'This is nice,' I say as I inspect the interior. 'And all the furniture is included?'

'That's right. Everything you see here can stay if you want it.'

'Excellent,' I say, because it will certainly save me a lot of money and trouble if I don't have to go furniture shopping once I have the keys to this place.

I take a seat on the edge of the bed to assess the firmness of the mattress. The thought runs through my mind that I might invite Miranda to take a seat beside me. But that might be a little too forward even for me, so I decide against it. The last thing I need is her calling me out as a creep and ending this appointment early, thus denying me the chance to hopefully become the owner once all the paperwork is sorted out in due course. But that doesn't mean I'm not planning on inviting her out for a drink once all the technicalities are out of the way, and who knows, with a bit of luck, Miranda might find herself back here again, albeit in a very different capacity to the one she is in now.

I hope she's wearing the same outfit then, too.

I smile to myself as I follow Miranda around the remaining upstairs rooms, but there is nothing in the rest of this guided tour that causes me to reconsider my plans, and by the time we are back downstairs again, I am ready to make my intentions clear.

'Well, I have to say that this is exactly what I'm looking for,' I begin, and Miranda looks pleased, no doubt already envisaging how she'll spend whatever commission she'll receive if she is successful in selling this place.

'That's wonderful to hear. I had a feeling you would like it. It really is a nice house.'

'Yes, it is. With that in mind, I'm going to put in an offer, and I'd like to move quickly on this.'

'Well, I can certainly try to make that possible, sir, depending on the seller accepting the offer, of course.'

'Of course. But I think they'll like it. I'm going to pay the full asking price outright with a single bank transfer.'

'Oh, so you're a cash buyer?' I watch as she struggles to keep her voice professional. 'Wow, I think the seller will certainly go for that.'

'I think so too.'

I smile at Miranda to show my confidence in getting what I want. But I also want her to know that I'm not just thinking about the house we are standing in. I'm thinking about her as well.

And I think she knows it.

'So, will you be living here by yourself?' Miranda asks, clocking the lack of a wedding ring on my finger, the wedding ring I removed and put in my pocket just before this appointment commenced.

'Possibly, although not all the time. This is primarily an investment opportunity.'

'I see. We do have a lot of clients who are buying second homes.'

'Yeah, and why not if they have the funds, right?'

I smile again before running a hand through my hair, a gesture designed really to flash the Rolex on my wrist and impress Miranda a little more.

'Do you enjoy your job?' I ask her, happy to prolong this conversation. I'm not due back at the office yet. I told Maria I was going for a meeting with a potential client, so she won't be wondering why I'm not at my desk beside hers.

'Yeah, I do. It has its moments, but overall, I like it.'

'Good. I think it's important to enjoy your job. Life would certainly be very dull if not, wouldn't it? And there's nothing worse than a dull life. We all need a little excitement in our day, don't we?'

I grin at Miranda, and she smiles back in agreement, and

while I feel confident enough to make a move on this woman right here, I tell myself to hold back until the ink is dry on the deal for this house.

Miranda assures me that she doesn't foresee any problems with my offer being accepted; she'll be in touch as soon as she has spoken to the seller and has some news. Then we leave the house, and as she locks the front door, I think about how I have finally ticked off an item that has been on my to-do list for some time.

I've been needing a place of my own so I have somewhere to take women back to. At the moment, my liaisons have been taking place in hotel rooms, but they always carry with them the fear that I might be spotted by somebody who knows me and could pass on the news to my wife that they have seen me in the company of an unknown female. That's why I decided that buying a modest, anonymous home would be a good investment, though I'm not talking in terms of a financial income. It's an investment in my love life, the one that exists beyond my marriage and the one that I will make sure my wife never finds out about.

I'm not a bad man. I just enjoy the company of women, namely lots of different women. I've been cheating on Maria since day one, but I'm not some monster, which is why I endeavour to ensure she never finds out. I don't want my wife to have her heart broken. Once I own this house, I will have the perfect place to spend time with any woman I like without any need for sneaking around in hotels and worrying about Maria finding something unusual on a credit card receipt.

I'll buy this house with one transfer using the money I have been funnelling out of our business into a secret bank account that Maria has no idea about.

I've been clever. I've thought it all through. This house is going to be a fantastic buy.

Lots of good times will happen here.
Now I just can't wait to get the keys.

20

WILLIAM

Looking down at the body by my feet, I'm aware of how this house hasn't quite ended up serving the purpose I bought it for. Sure, I've brought plenty of women here over the past few years and had more than my fair share of fun with them in the bedroom, not to mention all the other rooms in this house, the kitchen included. But there's nothing fun about what's happened in here tonight. Instead, all I am left with now is a major problem.

I have a dead body to get rid of.

But rather he be the one who has taken his last breath than me or my wife.

Maria.

She is still outside, locked in the trunk of my car. My first instinct is to try to grab the key fob from the dead man's pocket and run outside, where I can free my wife and make sure that she's okay. But then my second instinct tells me to hold off from doing such a thing just yet because, while it's certainly galling to see my wife imprisoned like that, I can't deny the benefit to me of Maria not seeing this house and knowing of its location.

My plan when I first suggested that David and I take a trip over here was for me to eventually get the upper hand and kill him, which I have of course done, but things became significantly less straightforward once he insisted that Maria come with us as well. I had no desire for her to see my illicit second home, even if I was running with the lie that it was actually where Adelina lived, which, of course, was complete nonsense.

But with Maria sitting beside me on the way over here, I'd been resigned to never being able to come back to this address again, as well as knowing that I was set to face uncomfortable questions about why exactly it was that I was so good at giving directions to get here.

However, when my wife unexpectedly tried to attract the attention of a passing motorist, I would have welcomed a stranger's intervention to help us evade David and his sinister intentions. But her efforts simply led to her being punished further by our driver. But once Maria was in the trunk, then I knew I'd been gifted the chance to keep my secret home as secret as it was designed to be. All I had to do then was figure out a way to convince David to let me explore the house with him, and once I had him alone, I knew I could take care of the rest.

And so it has worked out. He's dead, I've survived, and best of all, my secrets are still safe. Well, most of them anyway. Maria is now aware of the £50,000 payment I made to Adelina, which is regrettable, but not completely damning because I have explained it away with a reasonable excuse that I'm sure my wife will believe eventually if I stick to my story, which I fully intend to do. But she doesn't have to know about the fact that I actually lured David here to this house that I own under false pretences.

And she definitely doesn't need to know any of the other things that have taken place in my past, things that can never, ever come to light. There would be a lot more than my marriage at stake if that happened.

Staring down at David's lifeless corpse, it's hard to feel too sorry for him. Okay, so he was pretty much innocent with regard to Adelina and the charge of sexual harassment, and he didn't deserve me pinning the whole thing on him so he lost his job.

But, on the other hand, he held a knife to my wife's throat, so I'm hardly going to regret killing him. He had to go, and now he has, although just because he's dead, that doesn't mean that he isn't still a problem.

What to do with his body?

I have some ideas, but what matters here is the order in which I do things. I need to play this right so that Maria doesn't know how things are far worse than she could ever imagine. To achieve that, the answer as to what I need to do next is clear to me now.

I need to get my wife home.

Kneeling down beside David, trying not to spend too long looking into his eyes, which are staring lifelessly back at me, I fish around in his trouser pockets for the keys to the handcuffs but don't find them. But I do find the car keys, which is important if I'm to get out of here. It's tricky with handcuffs on, but I manage to scoop them out, and now that I have them, I can leave this house and go back to the car.

Leaving via the back door that we entered the property through after I 'accidentally' found the spare key in the garden, I use one of my elbows to hook the door handle and manoeuvre it so that the door closes behind me. I'll have to come back here soon and deal with the problem at the bottom of the stairs, but until then, I need this house to appear normal from the outside for this time of day. That means the doors are closed, and the lights are off.

The lights.

Damn it, I can see a yellow glow inside, so I get myself back into the house and flick the offending light switch off, plunging the house into darkness again and making it look like a place that would hold nothing of interest to anyone who happened to look in this direction.

The residents on this street will be used to this house being empty most of the time. After all, I'm hardly ever here, only usually calling by either in the middle of the day with one of my other women or letting myself in late at night with a woman I've met in a bar while Maria thinks I'm working or away on business. Therefore, they'll expect to see this place dark and unoccupied, so I'll make sure it looks exactly like it always does.

With the back door closed again, I rush around to the front of the house with the car keys in my hand, and I'm about to get in behind the wheel and start the engine when ...

'Oh, hello, Simon. I thought somebody was out here. I was just checking it was you.'

I recognise the voice behind me as belonging to Ken, a man from just up the street who has spoken to me a couple of times when he has rather annoyingly caught me here on one of my various dalliances. I gave him a fake name when I first met him, and like the irritating busybody that he is, he's remembered it while coming out to stick his nose into whatever my business might be on his street tonight. But I have a big problem here. I can't turn around and face him because if I do, then he will surely see the handcuffs around my wrists, and that will take some explaining.

'Oh, hey,' I say, glancing back over my shoulder but keeping the rest of my body facing away from him as I stand by the open door, longing to just get in and speed away. 'Sorry, I hope I didn't wake you. I just called around to get something, but I'm going now.'

'No, you didn't wake me. I'm a night owl, you see. I like to stay up late.'

Of course you do, you annoying twit. Why couldn't you be like everybody else and be in bed now, fast asleep and totally oblivious to the fact that you live so close to a murderer and a dead body?

'I see. Well, I'm just going now, so enjoy the rest of your evening.'

I try to leave then, going to get into the car and praying that Ken will just go back into his house. But he doesn't. He comes even closer to me ...

'This really is a lovely motor. Like the one James Bond drives, isn't it? Could I have a look at it? You don't mind, do you?'

Ken comes still closer, and that's when he sees them. The handcuffs on my wrists. And that's when his face drops because now he can't possibly believe that my visit here this evening is about anything even remotely resembling what could be considered normal.

'What's going on?' he asks as he stares at the shiny chunks of metal that bind my hands together.

Think fast, William. Think fast and think good.

'This is rather embarrassing,' I say as I bow my head to make it look like I've just been caught in an awkward situation, which I suppose I have, but Ken is going to get a very different story to the truth, that's for sure. 'I'm afraid you've caught me at a bad moment.'

'A bad moment?' he echoes in disbelief. 'Why on earth do you have handcuffs on?'

'I've been playing a game with someone,' I admit, still keeping my head down to appear sheepish. 'A lady friend.'

'Oh, I see,' Ken replies, and although I'm sure he doesn't really 'see', when I look up, he seems embarrassed for me.

'She likes to, how can I put it? Restrain me ...'

'Oh.'

Ken is really flustered now; he's actually hopping slightly from one foot to another.

'It's stupid, I know. But whatever turns her on, I guess.'

'Right. Say no more.'

Ken looks like he might be sweating, which is funny because I can feel a few beads of perspiration on my forehead too.

'So is she in the house now?' he asks, glancing over at the dark property in front of us, perhaps imagining a very different scene from the horrors that would greet him if he went inside.

'No, she's gone. But she likes to keep me handcuffed for a little while even after we've finished.' I force myself to meet his gaze, as if we were talking man-to-man. 'Just another part of her game.'

'So how do you get them off? Do you need some help? I've got some tools in my shed that could probably help break through them.'

'No, that won't be necessary. But thank you. She'll take them off me herself in the morning. She wouldn't be pleased if she found out I'd already got out of them. They're quite expensive, these handcuffs, so best not to damage them.'

He nods thoughtfully. 'But how can you drive in them?'

Good question, Ken. How about one for you. Why don't you mind your own bloody business?

'I'll be fine to drive. It's a little tricky, I'll admit, but this isn't the first time I've been in such an, ahem, unusual situation.'

Ken seems to blush at that. Then I tell him I really need to get going, but ask if he wouldn't mind keeping what

happened here between us so that none of the other neighbours find out.

'Yes, of course. You have my word. I won't tell a soul,' Ken
assures me. 'Just make sure you don't get stopped by the
police driving like that, or I'd imagine they'd want to put you
in their own set of handcuffs.'

'Good point. I'll make sure of that. Good night, Ken.'

*Not get caught. That's the whole aim of this, so bugger off and
let me get on with it.*

I think he's going to leave me alone then. He certainly
looks like he is because he turns to walk away, and I know it's
only a few seconds until he is back in his house, and I am off
this street and away.

And then we both hear it.

The muffled shout from the back of the car.

'What was that?' Ken asks.

'What? I didn't hear anything,' I try in vain.

'There it is again.'

Yep, Ken's right. *Maria just made another noise.*

What can I do? I can't open up the trunk and let her out.
Not only will Ken realise that I've been lying to him and that
something is seriously wrong here, but my wife will see the
house, and then she'll ask questions about David and
Adelina, threatening everything.

This is easily the longest night of my life.

But it's not over yet. *Unless ...*

'Oh, that? It's her,' I tell Ken, rolling my eyes.

'Who?'

'The woman I told you about. The one who put me in
these handcuffs. The *kinky* one.'

'Where is she?'

'She's in the trunk.'

'What?'

'It's part of our game.'

'You're kidding.'

'I'm afraid not.'

Now I'm really doing my best to look embarrassed while Ken just looks completely baffled. But I remind him that I've already sworn him to secrecy before I start the engine, drowning out any more noises from the back of the car.

'I really do have to go,' I tell him. 'Thanks for your discretion in this matter. Now, would you mind?'

I gesture to my door as if I want him to close it, and he actually apologises before he does as I wish. Then I manoeuvre my handcuffed wrists around enough so that I can release the handbrake, and then I'm on the move, driving carefully away with my restricted upper limbs resting on the steering wheel and working extra hard to keep it on track.

I stare at Ken in my rear-view mirror as I depart. He's standing in the middle of the road; then he shakes his head and goes back to his house.

I think he bought it. He must think that I'm a raving lunatic, but I think he believed me.

Now that's over with, at least for now, I can concentrate on what I was thinking about before he interrupted me, which is getting Maria home and then explaining to her exactly what has happened. But, just like I had to with Ken, to do it I'm going to need all my reserves of charm, my full repertoire of acting skills and, most of all, my canny ability to look somebody in the eye and tell them a bare-faced lie without them suspecting that I am not giving them the truth.

This won't be easy.

That's because my wife knows me better than anyone.

Or at least she thinks she does.

21

MARIA

I was starting to feel like I was never going to be let out of this prison of mine. It certainly didn't look good when I heard the engine start again and felt that the car was on the move. I was petrified that David had done something to William after something had gone wrong at Adelina's house, and now he was driving us somewhere before disposing of both of our bodies. But, really, it's hard to have any idea as to what might be going on in the outside world while curled up in a foetal position in the back of a car. The only hope I have of finding out is for the lid to be lifted and the outside to come into view again.

The engine has stopped, and I can hear footsteps approaching.

Is this it? Is David about to reach in and stab me over and over before dragging my bloodied corpse out to rot in a hidden location?

Are we in the woods? Is this going to be my final resting place?

Then the lid lifts, and I get the best surprise of my life.

It's not David looking down at me. It's my husband.

And he's smiling at me.

'William! Oh, my love!' I cry as I struggle to get out of the car, but it's almost impossible with my hands tied and my whole body rigid with cramp. William's hands are the same, but, together, we haul me out of the trunk, and as I stand beside him, I look around, wary of where David might be and what he might be planning next.

But I can't see him. He's not here.

What the hell is going on?

I notice that we're outside our house, on the driveway, and if it weren't for the fact we are both still wearing handcuffs, it could almost be as if nothing has happened here this evening.

'Where's David?' I gasp, refusing to believe that the man who has terrorised us for so many hours would just vanish without a trace and without hurting either of us.

'It's okay. He's gone. You don't have to worry about him anymore. Now, come on, let's get you inside. You need to sit down; you've been through a lot.'

William seems calm, as if he genuinely believes what he has just said, but it doesn't make any sense. He's right, I have been through a lot. But it's not over yet until I know everything about it.

'Gone? Gone where? What happened?'

'I made a deal with him.'

'What kind of deal?'

'I told him I'd give him money if he left us alone, and he accepted.'

'What? We offered him money earlier, and he said no. Why would he change his mind?'

'Because I offered him a lot.'

'How much?'

'It doesn't matter. He's gone. We're safe now.'

'William,' I persist, 'how much?'

The time for being surprised is over, and now I'm just being stern.

'A hundred grand.'

'You gave him a hundred grand?'

I'm staggered. The number is crazy. Huge. Certainly a lot for someone who was determined to kill us.

'I didn't want to, but I had to do something. Honestly, Maria, there was no other way.'

'What about Adelina? Did you go to her house? Was she there?'

'There is no house. I lied to stall him.'

'What do you mean?' I am finding it hard to make sense of any of this.

'I just needed a way to get us out of our house. He'd have killed us in our home. I figured if I could get us out, then maybe we could get help, or I could at least delay him enough to make him change his mind.'

'So where is Adelina?'

'I have no idea. Albania, I imagine.'

'So you haven't been having an affair with her?'

'Whatever gave you that idea? No, of course not!'

William looks incredulous that I would even suggest such a thing, but I had to ask him. I've been so paranoid about it ever since he admitted to giving her money.

'So where did you give him directions to?'

'Some random street across town. Nowhere specific. I was stalling him like I said.'

'But what happened? We were parked up for ages.'

'That's when we were talking.'

'Were you? I didn't hear you.'

'Maria, you were in the trunk. I'd be amazed if you heard anything at all. Time will have felt very distorted for you, too.'

I sigh and try to stretch out my back. I'm sure my husband's right, but this whole series of events still seems utterly perplexing. 'I'm just trying to make sense of all this.'

'I appreciate that, of course I do, but right now, it's late, it's been a hell of a night, and all I want to do is go inside and get these damn handcuffs off.'

'But, William,' I protest, 'we need to call the police!'

'What? Did you not listen to me? I gave David money to leave us alone, and he will now.'

'We can't just let him get away with what he's done! What if he comes back? What if he threatens the kids?'

'He won't, I promise you.'

'How can you know that? How can you have any idea what he might do? Before tonight, you didn't know he was capable of holding us at knifepoint!'

'Listen to me: David isn't coming back.'

'Why? Because of the money? Because I've got news for you, William. He could spend that and come back asking for more. What's to stop him?'

'I've apologised to him.'

'Apologised?' I echo, a little taken aback.

'That's right. I said sorry for firing him without a proper investigation. I know I screwed up. I know I took Adelina's word over his and didn't give him a chance to put his side of the story. And maybe I was wrong. Maybe David was innocent. Who knows, maybe Adelina was the guilty party in all of this and David was her victim.'

'That's not what you were saying earlier.'

'I know. But it's what I believe after spending half the night with David. I've seen how adamant he is. How desperate. I'm telling you, a guilty man wouldn't work so hard to try to clear his name. Only an innocent man would do that.'

'So now you think he's innocent?' I feel like I'm giving my husband a grilling here, but I just wish the pieces would slot into place more convincingly.

'Possibly. I don't know. But we'll never know because, like David said, Adelina has vanished. So I took a chance. I told him I believed him, and once I'd apologised, I made him the offer of the money, and this time, he was more receptive to it.'

I study my husband's face for any sign that he might be lying, but I can't see any. He's always so honest with me, and I feel like he's being the same now, which is important because after spending the last who knows how long in the back of this car, I'm completely dependent on his version of events.

'Look, he might be innocent, he might be guilty, but you have to admit we didn't exactly follow the rules when we got rid of him. Gallagher's is guilty of denying someone a fair hearing, and I don't want that becoming public knowledge, just like I didn't want the sexual harassment claim leaking out either. Everything I have done has been to protect us and our company, don't you see that?'

William looks so desperate for me to believe him that I almost do, but I just have a few more questions first.

'So, have you given him the money?'

'What?'

'The money. Have you already sent it to him?'

'Er, yeah. I did it on the app.'

'Which account did you use?'

'What does it matter?'

'I want to know.'

'I used one of our savings accounts.'

'Which one?'

'One of mine. Don't worry about it. It's my money, and it's been well spent to keep us safe.'

'But it's so much money!'

'I'm so sorry, but I just saved both our lives, our business and our future credibility. Can I get a little more appreciation for it, please?'

'Okay, I'm sorry,' I say, trying to calm him down. 'I'm just confused, that's all.'

'You're not the only one. I'm confused too, as well as exhausted, upset, angry, in shock. You name it. I thought I was going to lose you tonight.'

William looks on the verge of tears now, and I feel bad for interrogating him like this. But I have one more question, and then perhaps I can settle down a little bit.

'So David just left after you paid him?'

'Yes.'

'Did he say where he was going?'

'No, of course not. He might worry we'd just go straight to the police with that information.'

'And you won't do that?'

'I told you I won't.'

I nod. I guess that's it, then. This really might be over.

'Come on. Let's go in and figure out how to get out of these,' William says, holding up his handcuffs. He stomps to the front door, which luckily he finds unlocked after David thrust us out of it earlier. I'm about to follow him inside when I'm struck by something that really doesn't make sense.

If David let us go after receiving the money, why didn't he take the handcuffs off William's wrists? Would he really leave them on if they had come to some sort of deal?

I could ask my husband, and he might have a perfectly good explanation for it, but would it be the truth? Or does something not quite add up here?

As strange as it sounds, I feel a little wary about following William back into our house. That's because I'm afraid that he is keeping another secret from me, and it could be one that is much bigger than him secretly paying off Adelina. It could involve more than money. Or am I just being paranoid, the madness and sleepless terror of the evening taking its toll?

I eventually go inside and find William in the kitchen, where he is clumsily going through the drawers, trying to find something.

'The garage key!' he growls at me. 'Where the hell is it?'

'In the pot on the left, where it always his,' I tell him, and he tips it out and scoops it up.

'Follow me,' he barks, and when I do, he unlocks the garage, then nudges on the light. I watch while he picks up one of his power tools, an angle grinder he's used before for projects around the home like constructing the treehouse he made for the kids a couple of summers ago. But now he is going to use it to get the handcuffs off, and with the grinder plugged in, he sets it down on a workbench before turning it on and very carefully moving his wrists down in the direction of the spinning blade.

'William, don't; please be careful,' I cry, my heart pounding, but he keeps going, and there's a sudden snap of metal before he lifts his hands up and shows me that they are free. He grins widely before turning off the grinder and going in search of a less risky tool to help relieve me of my own cuffs.

He finds a hacksaw and instructs me to lay my hands down flat on the bench before he starts cutting, and while it hurts my wrists a little, he soon saws through the link between the cuffs, and I am free too.

'There, that's better,' he says. 'Now, how about we go and get a drink. I don't know about you, but I need something strong.'

He goes to leave the garage but pauses when he realises I'm not following him.

'Is everything okay?' he asks, and the question about why David didn't remove the handcuffs is on the tip of my tongue.

But I don't ask it.

I just want to enjoy that small taste of freedom.

Because I know I'll soon start worrying again that more than I might ever have imagined is far from how it should be in our world.

22

WILLIAM

Lying to my wife isn't something I'm proud of, but it has been a fixture of my marriage.

And never more so than now ...

But, as always, Maria has bought my lies about what happened with David yesterday, and with that problem dealt with, I have returned to the little house on Sharples Road to deal with my other problem.

As all dead bodies should be, David's is in the same place that I left it, at the bottom of the stairs, and while that's good, the fact that his eyes are still open is not. I really wish they would just close so I didn't have to feel like he was looking at me from beyond the grave. But the only way they'll shut now is if I shut them for him, and there's no way that's going to happen because it would mean having to touch his face, and I'm staying as far away from him as I can.

Only one person is going to be touching this body, and that's the man I have contacted to dispose of it.

The only name I have for him is the name he used on his advert, but like most things on the dark web, that secretive, murky and mostly illegal undertow of the internet, it's fake and chosen simply to ensure anonymity and evasion of the law.

TBone28.

I'll call him TBone for short.

My interest in the dark web was first triggered in the office one lunchtime a couple of years ago when I overheard two IT colleagues discussing it in the canteen. As I listened to their nerdy chat, I learnt how it's part of the internet that people access using anonymising software preventing anyone identifying them or tracking their activity as they seek out what my colleagues were calling 'onion addresses'. From what I gathered after joining their conversation by playing the part of the 'interested but technically challenged older guy', accessing this part of the internet itself isn't a crime. But once online in that underground version of it, there are plenty of opportunities to break the law.

Whether it's looking to buy firearms in countries where they are banned, launder money from criminal gain, engage in terrorist activities or a whole host of other illegal and immoral things, the dark web is home to all sorts of activity that will boggle the mind of the average law-abiding citizen.

It certainly boggled my mind when I figured out how to access it.

But I didn't need to do that until the first time I committed a crime.

You see, being with a dead body as I am right now isn't the first time I have crossed the line from innocent party to a guilty one. Just like this house I stand in, my past is a shady place, one that I'm not proud of but that exists anyway and can't be erased.

It's thanks to that past that I knew just the person to contact about my current difficulty.

I originally found his contact details on the dark web after purchasing the necessary hardware to access it, which not only included certain internet routers to keep my activity hidden but also a new laptop so Maria or the kids could never accidentally find out what I'd been doing if they went into my home office one day and started snooping around in places they shouldn't.

I'd been amazed at just what a person could shop for on the dark web. As far as online supermarkets go, it's surely the biggest and best in the world, or at least it is for a person who enjoys the more unsavoury aspects of life. There're people advertising all sorts of things, including and not limited to being willing to kill somebody for cash, being able to get any drugs a person might want, not to mention a whole host of depraved sexual services. But, most importantly for me, there were people who confirmed that, for a fee, they could make a dead body disappear.

I hadn't contacted anybody at the time I was browsing, mainly out of fear that they might have actually been under-cover police officers who were just waiting for an idiot like me to stumble into a world of crime before swooping in and arresting me. But I did note down a couple of potential contacts, because I never knew if I might need them in the future. And I'm glad I did because, thanks to David and the problem he now poses me, I certainly need somebody.

I need a body-removal expert.

I need TBone28.

It's dark outside, just as TBone told me it must be before he would make his arrival at the address I gave him after I contacted him earlier this morning. But as I stand by the curtains and peer out onto the quiet street, I'm still not convinced that I haven't made a terrible mistake and that soon this street will be filled with the flashing lights and sirens of police cars as they swoop in to arrest me for my crimes.

I'm praying TBone is who he says he is, although he's not said much in his correspondence. He just asked for the details of the body (sex, estimate of height and weight) before confirming the price, a cool £100,000, which I already knew because I'd seen it on his ads the first time I'd searched. And that's why I gave that same number to my wife as the figure I used to 'pay David off'.

She's expecting me to have given a hundred grand of our money to another person, so I will.

It just won't be the person I told her it was.

As I wait by the window and worry about whether or not I'm going to be back in handcuffs very soon, I think about Maria and Edward and Penny and how they'll all be at home now, my other home, getting on with their innocent, guilt-free lives, oblivious as to who the man they share a house with really is. I'm envious of their peace of mind and the fact that they can lay their heads down on their pillows every evening without minds riddled with stress about all the things they have done wrong in this world. It sure has been a long time since I have been able to do that. The problem with doing things wrongs once is that you can't ever undo them, which means the memory haunts you for ever. David might be gone now, just like all the woman in my past who weren't my wife have gone from my bed, but they remain stuck in my brain, tormenting me until the end of my days, whenever that might be.

And, depending on who this TBone character is, they might be ending a lot sooner than I might want.

A car arrives on the street then, approaching slowly,

cautiously, as if being operated by a driver who does not want to do a single thing that might attract the attention of anybody who could suspect him of being the kind of person who runs a body-disposal operation on the dark web. As the car comes to a stop, I feel relieved not to see any police markings on the side of the vehicle although I know perfectly well they could still be undercover, and they might just be waiting to come inside and see the dead body for themselves before they arrest me.

But I've come this far now, so I go to open the door and welcome in TBone, and when I do, I see that he is not quite what I expected. He's much younger than I anticipated, at least from what I can tell from his movements, which are springy and energetic. I can't see much of his face because it's disguised with dark sunglasses over his eyes, some stubble across his chin and a black hood pulled over his head. He looks to be wearing waterproof clothing, but then I realise what they really are, and they aren't to protect him from unexpected rain showers.

They're to protect him from blood.

I confirm that I am the person who contacted him and gave him this address before he asks me where the body is. I show him; then he carries in a small crate and stares at the corpse for several moments, all of which I spend waiting for him to tell me that the game is up and that I'll now be spending the rest of my life behind bars. I really wish I could have removed that risk and dealt with this body myself, but I tried that once before, and I vowed to never do it again. But when TBone speaks again, it isn't to tell me that he is an undercover cop. It's to tell me that he is going to get to work and that he'll let me know when he's finished.

I don't move at first, not because I want to watch him in action but because I'm still trying to process the craziness of the situation. But then TBone informs me that what he is about to do won't be pretty, and I see him remove some plastic sheeting from the crate as well as a handsaw, so I take that as a hint to leave quickly before I see things I'll never be able to forget.

Leaving the hired 'butcher' to his task, I go into the kitchen and stand awkwardly in there. I pour myself a glass of water from the tap and refresh my parched throat. I'm a bag of nerves, which I'm sure the man in the other room has noticed, but it's so far so good because he seems to be doing what I'm paying him for. And when he calls me back in an hour later, he confirms it.

I re-enter the room to find that David's body is no longer sprawled across my carpet at the bottom of the stairs. I'm guessing it is now in several pieces, all of which are wrapped and sitting inside the small black crate that TBone now closes by locking the interlinking lid.

'You'll want to change your carpets,' he instructs as he gestures at the area where David once lay. 'There's some visible blood that you can clean out, but it'll be the hairs that you'll never be able to fully remove. Best replace them.'

I nod to show that I understand before TBone asks me for the rest of the money transfer, and I take him over to where I have my laptop set up, the secret one my family don't know about; it's already connected to the dark web and, more specifically, the page where TBone's full payment can be made.

He watches me transfer the funds before nodding impassively, and as he returns to the crate, I can't help but wonder how often he does this kind of thing. It wouldn't take many dead bodies for him to accrue a 'retirement worthy' figure in his bank account, but then again, isn't even one body a body too many? I don't ask as he picks up the crate, demonstrating a strength that belies his diminutive frame, before he nods again to let me know he is leaving.

'Um, thanks,' I say awkwardly; then I ask, 'What happens now? I mean, with the body.'

'You really want to know?'

I think about it for a moment before shaking my head.

'I just want to know this won't ever come back to me,' I tell him.

'The only way it could come back to you is if you don't replace these carpets. But I know you'll do that because you seem like a sensible man. Goodbye.'

With that, TBone leaves, and I watch him load the crate into the back of his car before he gets in behind the wheel and drives away.

That's it. It's done. As simple as that.

I've discreetly and expertly managed the disposal of a dead body.

Now I need to go home and get into bed with my wife.

23

MARIA

'Mummy, are you okay?'

I wake up to the sound of my daughter's voice, and when I open my eyes, I see her standing beside my bed in her pyjamas, the concern on her pale face visible even through the gloom that tells me it's still dark outside.

'What? I'm fine,' I tell her, instantly reverting into 'Mum Mode' in which I can't ever let one of my children know that something might be wrong with me. But my daughter is too smart to be fooled, and she lets me know why.

'You were having a nightmare. Another one.'

Penny's summation is correct. I was having a nightmare, and she's also right in that it isn't my first one. I've been having them nearly every night, even more often than my little girl recently, which is saying a lot, but after what I've been through, I can hardly pretend I'm surprised.

I've been suffering from horrific nightmares ever since David broke into this house and almost killed me. Such an ordeal is clearly not something the average person has to deal with, so it's no wonder that my brain is struggling to function like it used to. It's also not helping that I haven't talked to anybody about what happened, other than the person who shared the experience with me of course, but even that hasn't helped me much. That's because William has said very little on the matter, preferring to keep reminding me that it is all over now and that things will get better if I just 'rest and give it time'.

But I wish I shared his optimism because, as far as I can tell, things aren't getting better. It's been a week now since that fateful night, and as well as struggling to sleep and emerging sweaty and distressed from sleep when I do drop off, I haven't yet been back to work. William told me to take as much time as I need and that he would cover for me in the office, which has been a big help, but in truth it is only dealing with the problem of keeping our everyday life ticking over. However, the problem of how to process a trauma like having a knife held to my throat in this very bedroom is not being dealt with, and until it is, I fear the nightmares won't end, and neither will the need for my daughter to get out of her bed to come and check if her mummy is okay.

It should be me going to her to soothe her after a bad dream, not the other way around. But right now, I do need my daughter's comforting touch, so I pull her in for a hug and give her a tight squeeze. She asks me then if it would be okay if she got into bed with me and slept in here, but I whisper to her that it would be best if she went back to her own bed because we don't want to wake Daddy. But then she points with a frown to the other side of the bed, and when I look, I see that William is not there.

'Oh,' I say, trying not to seem too surprised that I'm

sleeping alone. But I am surprised. The alarm clock beside me says that it's 01:52.

So why isn't William in bed?

I decide to go and investigate, pacifying Penny by allowing her to replace me on my side of the bed, so as she crawls under the duvet and spreads out on what must feel like a giant mattress to her, I leave the room to find out if William is somewhere in the house.

I discover him in his study, hunched over his laptop with a glass of whiskey on the desk beside him, and he startles when he sees me walk in.

'What are you doing up?' he asks with a slightly accusatory tone, as if it's okay for him to be awake in the middle of the night but not me.

'I had another bad dream. Penny came in to see me. She's in our bed now.'

'Oh, right.'

William takes a gulp of his drink as I stand in the doorway, shivering slightly. It's cold in here, although William doesn't seem to be feeling it.

'What are you doing?' I ask as I look at the lid of the laptop and wonder what might be on the screen on the other side of it, the side only my husband can see.

'Just surfing the web, you know,' comes the vague reply, and there's a brief awkward silence between us, one that seems to have infiltrated our relationship in the past week and that now rears its head several times a day.

'You should try to get some sleep,' I tell him. 'Penny's in our bed, but I can go in her room or on the sofa if you like.'

'No, that's okay. I'll take the sofa. You go and sleep with her.'

William doesn't look like he's ready to call it a night just yet, so I leave him and wander back through our dark, quiet house, my mind whirring away as I wonder what might be going on in my husband's brain at this time. He's never been an open book, so to speak, but he's definitely become even more private since what happened with David.

I wish he would talk to me. I wish he would tell me what he's thinking and how he's trying to process his own trauma from that night. That way, there could be a chance for the two of us to work through this together. To help each other. To heal each other. To maybe even come out stronger on the other side.

But that's not happening at the moment. If anything, it feels like we're drifting apart. But I know that's not all strictly down to the two of us still being in shock. It's also about the fact that I'm still struggling to believe everything William has told me.

I've tried my best, but I still can't believe that David would have just accepted the £100,000 pay-off. Sure, it's a huge sum of money, but I saw the look in his eyes when he was in this house. It was not the look of a man who could be bought off so easily, and I feel like I should know because I was the first one to offer him cash. Something else must have happened to change his mind, if his mind was changed at all.

But what?

Like every other night that I have spent dwelling on this, my mind comes up with only one potential solution to solve this whole mystery, or rather, one potential person.

Adelina.

She holds the key to all of this. She knows the truth. She knows whether she lied about David or whether he really did harass her, and she knows what that payment she received from my husband was really for.

I need to see her. I need to ask her. I need to get some answers.

But I can't do that if I can't find her.

I crawl back into bed beside Penny, who is already fast

asleep on my pillow, bless her. But I'm not going to be sleeping myself. Instead, I use my phone to conduct as wide and as extensive a search for any mentions of Adelina on the internet that I can. As always, the first and best port of call to 'stalk' somebody online is to type their name into various social media platforms, so I do just that. I might not be friends with her on any of these sites, but I might still be able to see her most recent updates on her profile page, and I certainly will be if she hasn't set her account to 'Private'.

Luckily she seems to be using her real name, and I find her easily on Instagram and begin carefully scrolling, expecting to see plenty of photos from her homeland, considering that's where everybody thinks she is now. Maybe a few images of her with family and friends or perhaps some scenic photographs of her country's famously stunning beaches and mountains. I know from chatting to Adelina that Albania enjoys a Mediterranean climate, so there may even be snaps of her relaxing outside a bistro in the sun.

But there are none. Instead, strangely, the most recent image is one I recognise. It's of Adelina sitting in the park near the office, enjoying an ice cream with a couple of colleagues. I recognise the photo because somebody submitted it for our monthly newsletter that HR sends out to all employees, and it featured in the 'It's Not All Work' section. But that was ages ago, wasn't it? It certainly feels like it. When I read the date below the image, I find out exactly when it was. It was seven months ago.

Before the sexual harassment claim. Before she left us. Before she disappeared and apparently 'went back home'.

What are the chances of her not posting anything since then? Looking at her older posts, it seems she was a fairly regular user, updating her feed regularly. But there's been nothing for a long time now and certainly nothing that would indicate she is back in Albania.

I decide to direct message her on this account. I don't want to scare her off, so I keep it light and vague, saying that I hope she is well, and I've just seen her profile after she came up as a 'Suggested for you'. But I do make sure to ask her where she is now because that's what I really want to know. Maybe she didn't go to Albania. Maybe she's still around here somewhere, and if so, perhaps I could meet her for a coffee. That would be great. It could certainly go some way to easing my worries.

But despite sending the message and staying up all night, refreshing my account to see if she has seen it, there is nothing. I figure she was just asleep, but as the next day wears on, there is still no response.

Like her photos, everything has gone quiet.

Where are you, Adelina?

Are you okay?

Or has something happened to you?

24

WILLIAM

Another busy morning of work has just come to an end, and now I'm leaving the office for a quick workout at the local gym. Exercise is something that I've had a love-hate relationship with throughout my life, but I'm currently in the middle of a 'love' phase and keen to get fit, not just for myself but for the many women in my life.

I know the ladies tend to prefer muscles over beer bellies, however fat the wallet might be, so I'm making the effort, for my wife, and for the women I take back to Sharples Road. I certainly can't complain about my sex life, but I know that getting fit will only improve my performance in the bedroom, so while I have to suffer a little bit of pain in the gym three times a week, the reward is even greater pleasure when the time comes to slip between the sheets with whichever lucky lady I'm with that night.

I have my gym bag in hand, and it has a packed lunch inside it, one that Maria made for me this morning because she is fully supportive of my wish to live a healthier lifestyle for her and the kids. I didn't tell her that instead of chicken, rice and broccoli, I'd have preferred a beer and a burger; instead I just thanked her for kindly caring about my diet before I shoved the lunchbox into my bag and said I couldn't wait to eat it. I was so 'excited' about it that I almost forgot to take it out of the canteen fridge before I left, but I have it now, along with a spare change of clothes and a pair of trainers, so I'm all set for action.

The treadmill isn't going to know what hit it.

But then I leave the office and see something that makes me feel more like I don't know what's just hit me. That's because it's a person I didn't expect to see, a face from my recent past who assured me that I would never have to see her again.

Whom I paid to remove herself from my life.

Yet she's walking across the car park towards the office.

But why is she here?

Why is she breaking the terms of our agreement?

'What the hell are you doing here?' I ask while urgently looking around to see if anybody else is in this car park. I'm glad to see that there isn't, but this is a busy office with lots of comings and goings, so it's only a matter of time before somebody does pass through here, and when they do, I want Adelina to be gone so they don't start with any polite chit-chat about how she's been and what she's been up to.

'I've come to talk to you,' she replies calmly, but while she is acting like everything is okay, there is evidence in her appearance that things are not quite right with her. She's lost some weight, which wouldn't normally be a problem for anybody, but she was always slender to begin with, and now she's looking gaunt. She looks very tired too, with the dark circles under her eyes a giveaway of restless, sleepless nights. While she's not exactly haggard, she's not looking anywhere near as pretty as she did the night I first made a pass at her.

'Talk to me? About what? We have nothing to talk about.'

'Yes, we do.'

'Then why didn't you phone me? I could have come and met you. Why are you here?'

'Because this is a workplace issue, so where else would I want to discuss it?'

'A workplace issue?' I'm not even pretending to keep my cool at this point. 'What the hell are you talking about?'

'I've changed my mind. I don't want your money, and I'll give it back, every single penny of it. I don't want to be paid off. I'd rather the truth came out about what really happened.'

I look at her, aghast. All of that sounds utterly terrifying to me.

'We made a deal!' I hiss, pleading with her to reconsider. 'You took that money and said you would never talk about it again!'

'I just told you. I changed my mind.'

'But you can't just do that. That wasn't part of the agreement. This wasn't a business deal. There wasn't a cooling-off period, for God's sake!'

'That's irrelevant.' She shrugs, unmoved. 'I'm not going to apologise. You're the one who should be apologising. To me, to your wife and to David, the man we have ruined.'

'Apologise?' I almost shout. 'Don't be stupid! I'm not the only one who has done something wrong now. You have too. You made the false claim. You cost David his job, not me. If you tell the truth now, you'll be in all sorts of trouble. He could sue you!'

'I don't care,' she says, her eyes glinting. 'I just want to do the right thing! I want to do what I should have done at the time. I want to expose you.'

The way Adelina says that last sentence chills my entire body, but there's no time to feel sorry for myself because I hear the automatic doors of the office slide open behind me. Somebody is about to come out.

'Quickly, come here. Let me just understand all of this before you go inside and ruin me.'

I grab Adelina's arm and lead her around the side of the building where we are out of view of the car park. She tries to pull away, but I'm not going to let her go.

'Please don't do this. What can I offer you? Do you want more money? I can get it for you if you do, but you have to promise you won't come back again.'

'I don't want your money. I just told you I'm going to give it back.'

'Are you crazy?'

'No. But I can't live with the guilt of what we did to David. And I can't live with the thought of Maria having no idea what her husband is really like.'

It's obvious that there is no changing her mind. And that's why I react instinctively, choosing actions over words.

I move my hand up from where it is gripping her arm to grip her throat. My left hand joins it, and between them, they begin to strangle Adelina, squeezing her throat tighter and tighter as she gargles and gasps, desperately trying to suck in the oxygen that I am now depriving her of.

She wriggles and bucks, tries to kick out at me, but I remain steadfast and refuse to change course now. I'm fully committed to silencing her once and for all.

And then it's done.

I feel her body relax.

I see her eyes roll back before they close.

And when I loosen my grip, she falls at my feet, her body

landing hard on the concrete, her arms splayed out to the sides, her legs folded awkwardly, and her mouth that could have done so much damage to me if I had let her speak the truth now grotesquely twisted.

I'm sweating, and I haven't even made it to the gym yet, but I haven't got a moment to waste.

I need to hide this ruined body before anybody walks down the side of this building.

I'm grateful that I didn't suggest we install security cameras at the side of the office now. I'm also grateful that I suggested we buy this building that is right next to a park because it's the trees and bushes of that park that can help me conceal Adelina's body, for now at least.

I grab her limp hands and drag her across the short concrete path before moving into the shrubbery and quickly locating a suitable bush to hide the body in. I'll have to come back soon, once darkness falls, to move her elsewhere because it is in real danger of being discovered by a dog here, but I can't do much in daylight, so this will have to do for now.

The afternoon I spend in the office is easily the longest of my life, and I find it impossible to concentrate on anything other than what I did at lunchtime. I spend one horrendous ninety-minute meeting staring out of the boardroom window, looking down at the green grass and the tall trees of the park and thinking about how there is something very sinister lurking within its borders. I also see all the people walking around in the park, some of them children, and think about how they have no idea that they are treading so close to something that could give them nightmares for the rest of their lives.

It feels like the working day will never end, but it eventually does, and as my employees drift out of the office, getting into their cars and driving away to go and spend their evenings doing whatever fun things they might have planned, I know I have the night from hell ahead of me. But first, I have to convince Maria that I need to stay and work late tonight, and while she is disappointed to hear that because we already had plans to have a nice dinner together and watch a couple of episodes of our favourite TV show once the kids were in bed, I tell her that I don't have a choice.

She leaves me to go and tend to matters at home, and once she is out of the office and darkness has fallen, I only have one more obstacle in my way. *The security guard who patrols reception.* I need to get him out of the way to give me enough time to back my car up to the building and drag Adelina's body into the back of it.

Using all my charm and wit, I convince the guy that I need a big favour from him because I'm in a bit of a mess, and only he can help me now. I tell him I have an important conference call with a client in New York that I need to be on in five minutes, but my quandary is that I have forgotten to buy my wife an anniversary present, and the only thing I can get her now is flowers from the local supermarket. But that closes in ten minutes, so I'll never make it if I have my call. With that in mind, could the security guard go out and choose the best bunch of flowers they have for me?

He agrees, no doubt helped by the fifty-pound note I give him for his troubles – and discretion; *not a word to Mrs G,* I add with a wink – and while he's out of the way, I run to my car and reverse it as near to the side of the building as I can. Then I rush back to the bushes where I left Adelina and find her colder and a little stiffer than when I last handled her as I drag her towards my car and haul her into the trunk.

It's exhausting work, but I get it done, giving thanks for all those gym sessions, and with her safely stowed away, I return my car to the same parking spot in the otherwise empty car park before the guard returns with an extravagant bouquet of flowers.

'Thank you. You're a lifesaver,' I tell him before apologising that my conference call actually got cancelled at the last minute so I could have gone myself after all. But he's not too bothered about that now he's fifty pounds richer for ten minutes' work, so I bid him goodnight and scurry back to my car with the flowers in hand.

I speed away, glad to put some distance between myself and the place where I officially became a murderer, but I'm not on my way home just yet. I'm heading for the forest on the outskirts of town, the one that I know is big enough to hide a body in the hope that it could go undetected for many, many years, if not for ever.

As I reach the forest, I slow down to navigate the small dirt tracks that cut through it. I wonder how many other people might have come here in the past with similar objectives to mine. I like to think that this is a place where bird-watchers come to see what they can spot in the trees and where children occasionally ride their bikes under the proud gaze of their parents, but there are surely more sinister activities that have gone on here too, like people hiding things they never want anybody else to find.

I initially think about trying to conceal Adelina's body in the dense undergrowth out here in the centre of this sprawling forest, but then I remember that there is a small lake in the middle of these tall trees, and I decide that might be the best place to dispose of a corpse.

Reaching the body of water, I watch the moonlight shimmering on the surface before I get out of my car and begin the process of dragging Adelina's body down to the water's edge. Then I start filling her pockets with as many rocks and stones as I can find, making her as heavy as possible so that she sinks to the bottom of this lake and never floats up to the top again.

I wade out with her weighed-down body until I am up to my waist, and as I start to feel her sinking, I know this is almost over.

I should just let go of her. Let her drift down into the murky depths. Forget all about her, get out of here and go home and shower away my sins. But before I do that, I take one last look down at her face, and I instantly regret it.

It's a sight that will haunt me for ever.

Just before it disappears into the water, I see Adelina's once beautiful, lively face twisted in horror. The image burns itself onto my retinas and into my brain; it's one I'll see in many a bad dream over the course of my life.

But with the body settling at the bottom of the lake, I return to my car and change into the spare clothes in my gym bag, thankful that I have them because they provide me with a much better option than arriving home in a sodden, stinking suit. Then I spend some time sitting in the driver's seat just staring out at the lake and thinking about what I have done. It's torture, but I engage in it anyway, punishing myself because I know that I deserve it. It's hard to believe that a woman is underneath the water now, a woman who loved every minute of her life before I snuffed it out in one panicked moment.

I never expected to kill somebody, nor did I ever think I was capable of it, but now that it has happened, this experience has taught me one thing. If, for whatever reason, I have to kill and cover it up again, I will get somebody else to deal with the body. Disposing of Adelina's corpse was definitely the worst part of this whole exercise.

Killing was actually easy. *Hiding the evidence was not.*

Still, hopefully, I'll never do something like this again. But if I do, I'll need help in dealing with the consequences. An expert to take the body. What's that thing the IT guys talk about sometimes? The dark web? Maybe I could find somebody on there to help me if I need them in future. But that's a big if.

I really hope I'm never backed into a corner and forced to fight my way out of it like I have done today.

I eventually make it back home, where I find Maria waiting up for me. She frowns when she sees me enter the living room in my gym clothes, but I explain it away by telling her that I felt so stressed after a busy day of work that I needed to let off some steam on the treadmill at the gym. She isn't mad at me for choosing a healthy way to relax, pleased that I've opted for exercise over hitting the bottle, as I so often do when things get tough. But then she tells me that she would appreciate it if I didn't stay out so late because it's not fair to leave her to do everything around the house when she has been busy at work herself all day as well.

I apologise and agree with her, wishing that I could just get into bed and bring this day to an end. But before that happens, I remember something, and it's something that I think will go some way to making my wife forgive me for being out late this evening.

I return to my car and collect the item before coming back inside and presenting it to her, upon which she smiles and tells me how sweet I am.

It's the flowers I sent the security guard out to get while I moved Adelina's body. It seems they have served a second purpose today. Not only did they help me remove a potential witness earlier, but they have got me back in my wife's good books. Now Maria is kissing me, pulling me into her, making it clear that she has a workout of her own to put me through now that I'm home from the gym.

I'm exhausted and stressed out, though I insist on a quick shower to wash the lake off me before I find the strength to make love to her. But I make sure to keep my eyes open the whole time we are together. That's because I know that when I close them, it won't be her face that I see.

It will be Adelina's and how she looked just before she slipped beneath the surface.

25

MARIA

I'm still finding it tough to sleep, which is why I'm absent from the office again today. William is very sympathetic to my plight and is eager for me not to rush back into things until I feel I am over that dreadful night with David, but he has also mentioned we have a couple of important meetings coming up next week, and it would be good if I could be there.

I get it. He is thinking of the business, as well as most likely hoping things will quickly go back to normal. But it remains to be seen if that is even possible because I'm struggling to think of anything but Adelina and what might have really happened between her, my husband and the man who almost killed me.

Adelina did not reply to the message I sent her on social media. As far as I know, she hasn't even read it: there's no notification under the message. But, not to be deterred, I decided to try to contact somebody else. I have reached out to a woman who has been tagged in several of Adelina's older photos, a woman who is clearly a friend of hers and who might be able to help shed a little light on Adelina's whereabouts since she left my company.

Her name is Tess, and after messaging her and telling her that I was an old colleague of Adelina's who had been trying to reach her without any luck, I suggested we meet up for a quick coffee. Tess seemed unsure at first, and the time it took for her to reply to my messages increased the more frequently I contacted her, but I was eventually able to persuade her to see me. Now I'm walking into the café that I selected as the meeting point and praying that Tess will be here. She's my best chance at learning more about my old employee.

I'm early, so I face a nervous wait when Tess doesn't appear at the time we agreed, but she finally walks in seven minutes late, and recognising her easily from her photos online, I wave her over. She's lucky she isn't here for a job interview because her lateness would have already counted against her, but as it is, I'm just glad to see her, and as she takes a seat at my table, I thank her for coming.

'I'm not really sure what you want me to do,' Tess admits as she looks around the café at the people at the other tables, people who are presumably good friends and are under more normal circumstances than we are.

'I just want to talk about Adelina,' I say, smiling to try to put her at ease. 'Like I said, we used to work together, and I considered her a friend. But I'm not sure what happened to her after she left, and I was wondering if you had some answers. You two seemed pretty close from the photos I saw.'

'Close? We were best friends.'

'Were best friends?'

'Yep. But not anymore.'

'So, what happened?'

'She stopped replying to my messages. She ghosted me, if you will.'

I've heard that term a few times in the TV crime dramas I like. I wouldn't use it myself, but I know it means Adelina essentially ceased all communication with Tess without any explanation as to why.

'Isn't that weird?' I say, wondering how hurt Tess might feel about all this.

'Well, yeah. But I guess she didn't think we were as close as I did.'

I nod, wanting to seem sympathetic before prying a little further. 'When was the last time you spoke to her?'

'Erm, I don't know. Around four months ago, I think.'

'So she'd left her job by then.'

'Yeah.'

'And did you talk about why she left?'

Tess nods. 'Yeah, a lot. It was a big deal for her.'

'I guess so,' I agree as neutrally as I can. 'What did she tell you?' I'm on tenterhooks to know, but we have to pause the conversation so the waitress can take our order.

Tess takes a deep breath, holds my gaze. 'She told me she had been harassed and that the guy had been fired, but she didn't want to work there anymore.'

'Okay. Do you remember anything else?'

'She mentioned a pay-off.'

I raise my eyebrows in response to that, and Tess continues.

'Yeah, she didn't say how much, but I guessed it was a decent amount because she didn't seem in a rush to find another job.'

'And how would you describe her mood around this time.'

'Her mood?'

'Yeah, was she happy? Sad? Troubled?'

'I don't know. She was quieter than normal, but I didn't think it was weird because she'd obviously been through something horrible with the harassment. I was glad it was behind her. Or at least I thought it was.'

'What do you mean?'

'Well, I guess it wasn't if she ended up leaving.'

'Leaving where?'

'Here. She went home to Albania, I presume.'

'You presume?'

'Well.' Tess hesitates for a moment, as if challenging her own assumptions. 'But where else would she go?'

'I don't know. She could have gone anywhere. Or she might have stayed.'

'No, impossible. We were best friends.' I catch a shadow of hurt – or maybe disappointment – darken her eyes for a second, as she remembers. 'Honestly, if she was still in town, I'd definitely know about it.'

Our drinks arrive then, and I hope I can come here again one day and enjoy a coffee under more normal circumstances.

'Don't you think it's odd how she just disappeared?' I ask as we stir sugar into our coffees. 'I mean, she just stopped talking to you, her best friend, and stopped updating her social media. No photos. No words. Nothing.'

'Of course it is,' Tess confirms. 'I actually went to the police station one night to tell them I was worried about Adelina and see if they could find out where she was.'

'Really,' I exclaim. I wasn't expecting her to say this, and I'm intrigued. 'What did they say?'

'They seemed curious at first until they found out where she's from. Then they just said she must have gone home and really weren't interested. They said it's fairly common for people to just up and leave.' She looks at me, unconvinced, then shrugs. 'I suppose it is possible that she returned to her home country. But, you know, it's not like they don't have Instagram in Albania, so ...'

'Do you have a contact for anybody there?' I ask. 'A family member or a friend we could ask to see if Adelina is with them?'

'No, nothing,' Tess replies and her words sound so final, like yet another dead end for my investigation. I'm left with nothing to do for the moment but sip my coffee and puzzle over which other doors I might try to open. But Tess speaks again before I have a chance to ask her anything else.

'Why some many questions?' she asks as she drains the last of her coffee. 'Why are you so bothered about where she might be?'

'Well, naturally, I'm just a bit concerned about her.'

'Yeah, but why?'

I consider telling Tess about how the man Adelina accused of harassing her spent a night terrorising me and my husband, but I know that I can't. William swore me to secrecy, insisting that was part of the agreement he'd made with David. But I do admit to being more than simply Adelina's ex-colleague.

'I was actually your friend's former boss,' I venture.

'So you were in charge when she was harassed?' Tess asks in a sharp, slightly accusatory tone, as if I should have foreseen any trouble and headed it off before it occurred.

'Well, yes, my husband and I were. But we had no idea that something like that might happen in our workplace. It was the first time such an incident had occurred there.'

'Your husband?' And, again, Tess's tone is abrupt, wrong-footing me. 'Is he called William by any chance?'

'Yeah, why?' I ask, nervous now. The look on Tess's face is far from amenable.

'Adelina mentioned him a couple of times.'

'Oh.' And I can't help but dig deeper; it's not often I get a chance to hear an employee's side of the story. 'What did she say about him?'

Tess hesitates, but I urge her to enlighten me.

'She said he was a bit of a flirt. Always made the effort to call by her desk and start a conversation. And he was a bit cheeky at staff parties when he'd had a drink. He complimented her a few times.' She lowers her gaze, a little embarrassed. 'She said he sometimes acted like he wasn't married.'

Tess's words sting. Part of me wants to get angry and tell her she has no idea what my husband is like, that she can't take the word of another woman. But another part of me feels like this is another secret he had, just like he kept the payment he made to Adelina secret. Once again, I'm consumed by paranoia that something was going on with those two, something that ran much deeper than a connection between co-workers.

I've spent this conversation with Tess trying to find out more about Adelina. But now I feel like the person I need to be asking about is the man I married.

What else don't I know about him?

What else do other people see that I don't?

What else could he be hiding from me?

26

WILLIAM

I love it when a business meeting goes well. It gives me such a great sense of satisfaction, and today, I've just finished leading a meeting with three potential clients, all men who were eager to test me and my company's credentials before deciding whether or not to award us the contract we've been hoping to land. But I feel like I passed that test and was the epitome of confidence as I sat at the head of the boardroom table and answered every single question in as much detail as they needed me to.

While I've certainly had a few hair-raising moments in my personal life recently, I pride myself on never getting flustered in my professional one, and now this meeting has come to an end, I'm congratulating myself on another job well done. I'm also enjoying the fact that, despite everything I've been through – with Adelina, with David, and with the differing means by which I disposed of their bodies – I feel like I am back to my normal self again. I'm not as stressed, which means I'm sleeping better and drinking less, all of which means I'm able to do what I do best and lead this company towards another profitable quarter.

I'm also doing good things at home, picking up the slack that has occurred ever since Maria has been less resourceful than usual. She's taking a little longer than I am to get over what we both went through, but I've let her know that she should take as much time as she needs and that I'll keep things ticking over both at work and at home. I've been cooking dinner for the kids, I've been tucking them into bed, and I've even been sighted around the house with the vacuum cleaner and a feather duster. In other words, despite the recent troubles, I'm a fully functioning husband and father, giving my wife no reason to think that I'm anything other than the perfect man she believes she is lucky to have married.

Leaving the meeting room with a spring in my step, I'm making my way back to my office for what should be a slightly easier next hour of my day, during which the hardest thing I'll have to do is answer a few emails. But before I do that, I make sure to pay a visit to the HR office to say hello to the person currently behind the desk there.

'Hey, Ronnie. How's it going?'

The latest person to hold the title of HR manager at Gallagher's looks up from his work and smiles when he sees me.

'All good, Mr Gallagher,' he says. 'Everything okay at your end?'

'Great,' I tell him with a big smile before looking at the photo of him and his family that sits on the edge of his desk. 'How are the kids? I hope they're well?'

Ronnie confirms that they are indeed well, and I tell him that's great news. Then I joke that I don't want to see him working too late tonight because I've noticed that he's been putting in longer hours recently.

'Your probation period is over now, and you passed it with flying colours, so you can relax a little,' I say with a grin.

He thanks me before I leave, no doubt relieved that he doesn't have to stay as late at the office as he has been doing ever since he got this job a couple of months ago. As Becky's replacement, he has clearly been eager to make a good impression, but he's not the only one who has been working hard to be seen in a positive light. That's because I always make it a priority to be on extremely good terms with whoever is in the HR department these days, having learnt that it came in super handy last time around.

Being friendly with Becky meant that it was much easier to steer her towards the conclusion I was looking for with the David and Adelina harassment 'investigation'. I have no doubts that if I hadn't been on such good terms with her, then she would have been more likely to conduct a more thorough investigation, and that would have been very problematic for me. As it was, I convinced her to go along with my decision to terminate David's employment, and while I could see that she was uneasy about the speed of it all, she did as I asked.

But it was perhaps that uneasiness that led her to hand in her notice not long after the whole episode was over, and while I pretended to be surprised at that, as well as upset to learn that she wanted to go, in reality I was delighted that she was looking to move on. With Becky gone, that meant that everybody involved in that harassment claim had now left the company in one way or another, and to me, that cemented my belief that I could keep the whole thing under wraps and the truth buried for ever.

And so it has proven. But to make absolutely sure Becky never felt like voicing her concerns to anybody after she departed, I sent her a final bonus not long after she left. This came under the guise of me wanting to give her an extra, personal thank you for all the excellent work she did for us as part of my company.

And, rather unsurprisingly, she didn't reject it.

While I am not planning on ever having to need to persuade HR to break a few rules and effectively bail me out of another harassment scenario in the future, I do think it is wise to keep Becky's replacement close should I ever need him firmly on my side one day.

As I reach my office and close my door, I can't help but smile to myself because I really am good at what I do. I manage people. I control them. And I get my way. *Always.* At this point, considering what I've been through and all I've overcome, it's hard to imagine a time when the tables could be turned and things could go wrong for me.

Is it on the horizon?

No, not as far as I can tell.

It's just plain blue skies all the way now. Not a storm cloud in sight.

That's because I'm a winner.

And everybody else in this life is a mere pawn in my game.

27

MARIA

I surprised William this morning by telling him that I was ready to go back to work. He asked me if I was sure and said that I could take another couple of days if I needed to because the important meetings he would like me to attend aren't quite here yet, but I told him that it was time for me to get back into my normal routine. He had smiled then before giving me a hug and saying it was good to have me back. I played along with it, but all the while, I just kept thinking about how he had no idea.

He had no idea that I wasn't back at all.

If anything, it would be a new me who would be returning to work, a me who was no longer naïve enough to believe everything that came out of my husband's mouth.

The reason I'm so eager to get back to the office isn't because I am over what happened with David. It's because I want to keep a closer eye on William, and the best place to do that, other than at home, is in the workplace we share together. But unlike all the other times when I watched him in the office, blinkered by my love for him and a belief that he was perfect in everything he did, I will now watch him in a much more sceptical way. I'll be looking for flaws, faults and, most importantly, mistakes. But I don't just have to look at him to try to spot those. I can also look into the company accounts. I want to see the details of that pay-out he gave to Adelina before she left, as well as check that there haven't been any other ones that might have slipped through without me being made aware of them.

I receive a warm welcome as I arrive in the office on my first day back, and everybody seems genuinely pleased to see me, from the security guard in the reception to all the members of the sales team and even Ronnie, our new HR manager, whom I wasn't quite convinced about during the interview process, but who William convinced me was the best candidate for the role. Once again, as always, I went with my husband's decision. I thought it was for the best, and that was because I believed he only ever had the best of intentions in mind. But we'll see about that.

The day goes by rather slowly. I'm not helped by the banging headache that strikes just after eleven o'clock, nor by the constant imaginings of David in my home putting that knife to my throat, which are haunting me; thoughts of him seem automatic now that I'm here in a place he used to work. I'm actively avoiding walking past the desk he once sat at, as if just being anywhere near would be enough to trigger a panic attack. Maybe it will, or maybe I'm being paranoid, but I won't risk it either way.

I keep my eyes on William for as much of the day as I can, watching him at his desk opposite mine and asking myself what might be going on in that head of his. I think about what Tess said about how Adelina described him as a flirt who sometimes acted as if he weren't married, and when I do, I feel an anger rise inside me that makes me want to run over to his desk, slap him and ask him if it's true. But I don't do that because then he would ask me how I even came to know such a thing, and then I'd have to tell him that I spoke to one of Adelina's old friends, which would surely tip him off as to the fact that I'm not letting things lie yet. So I say nothing, doing my best to act normal all day until it's time for him to suggest we log off our laptops and head to my parents' to pick up the kids before taking them home for a pizza and a movie night. That's when I do something that would not be considered normal for me.

'No,' I tell him, my voice resolute. 'I'm going to stay late and work tonight instead.'

'I'm sorry, did you not hear me? I suggested a takeaway and movie night with the kids. What part of that doesn't sound good?'

'It all sounds good. I've just got a lot of work to catch up on. My inbox is crazy.'

'It's your first day back. I don't think you should overdo it.'

'I'm not overdoing it.'

William raises a sceptical eyebrow at me, but I smile to let him know that I'm fine.

'I told you I just want to get back to normal, and for me, working hard is normal,' I say, really wanting to convince him to leave me alone here.

'Okay, if you're sure.'

'I am.'

William shrugs before walking over to give me a kiss.

'Don't stay too late, all right? I'll save you some pizza.'

'You're the best.' I kiss him back, hoping my words might still be true but feeling more unsure about them than I ever have.

William leaves the office then, and I feel strange for a

moment, as if I'm relaxing a little, which only tells me that I must have been feeling tense all day in the presence of my husband. I know that's not normal, but it is how I feel, and I can only hope it's a feeling that won't last. But to get to that point, I need to keep looking into things. So I start to do just that again.

Accessing the accounts files on the company server, I begin the tedious process of looking for any potentially irregular past transactions. It doesn't take me long to spot the £50,000 payment to Adelina, and I curse myself for never paying this much attention to the accounts before, but, as William reminded me at the time, I never got involved in that side of things. I do wonder how he got it past our finance manager; although being the boss, William can get anything past anybody here; plus I'm sure he might have added a little extra to his particular bonus as a way of saying thanks for keeping it from me.

All of the other transactions I find seem normal until I come across a £5,000 payment that was made a couple of months ago. When I look to see who it was made to, I see the name.

Becky O'Connell

'What's this for?' I ask out loud as I study it. The date catches my eye. This payment was made after she left the company. Why would William give her money after she'd gone? And why is this yet another example of him keeping something from me?

He told me the payment to Adelina was the only one he'd kept secret, but now I've just found him to have lied again. Is that how gullible he thinks I am? He believes that I wouldn't even suspect him of deceiving me. He believes that I wouldn't think to check the company records? Maybe he has been playing me for a fool for such a long time that he doesn't imagine I'll ever catch him out in his lies.

Maybe I'm only just starting to wake up to the extent of his untruths.

I want more information about this one, and I know the best place to find it. Becky. She asked me for a reference after she left, and I provided her with a good one, which she used to land herself a great position at another company across town. Knowing where she works makes it a lot easier to ask her some questions than it was to find out what little I do about Adelina.

I'll go to Becky's new office and speak to her this week. I'll ask her why she received money from William after she'd left here. And then I'll wait and see what she has to say.

It could be good.

Or, like everything else that seems to be happening lately, it could be bad.

28

WILLIAM

I'm back enjoying life with my favourite thing. It might be the only thing in this world that truly understands me. It's my expenses card.

Tonight, I am certainly racking up the expenses.

I've been wining and dining potential clients all afternoon, and now we're running into the early evening, but this 'business meeting' is showing no signs of slowing down yet despite the fact that we haven't actually talked about anything even remotely resembling business for the last couple of hours. We're in a rooftop bar that offers incredible views of the city, a city that I never tire of venturing into when town life gets a little dull. As I look out over the bright lights of this sprawling urban landscape, I feel the same as I always do when I'm at the heart of a place with such energy. I feel opportunity all around me. And there almost certainly is, but not just in the business deals I could make. I'm also talking about the beautiful women here, women who are looking for a good time.

Women who are looking at me right now.

I raise my glass and smile at the pretty waitress to let her know I'm ready to order another round, and she acknowledges me before making her way past the various tables in here to get to my own. When she reaches us, I refrain from simply telling her our drinks order and, instead, ask her how her night is going. I also make sure to use her name, Stephanie, as indicated by the badge pinned to her smart uniform.

'It's going okay, thank you,' she replies as she smiles at me and the other men at my table. I notice all those men are smiling back and have stopped whatever conversations they might have been taking part in, clearly more interested in her than anything one of them might have been saying. And why shouldn't they be? Stephanie is gorgeous.

She's probably at least twenty years younger than us men, which is unlikely to detract from the attraction, but I'm not going to do anything that emphasises the fact that I'm old enough to be her father. Rather, I'm going to make sure I come across as fun, flirty and, most of all, financially free.

'That's good to hear, Stephanie. Life's too short not to enjoy yourself, isn't it?' I reply before getting my wallet out and opening it up so Stephanie can see the crisp twenties lined up in there and presume I can use them for tips. Then I hand her my expenses card while asking her what her favourite drink is.

'Oh, an Aperol spritz.' She laughs. 'I love them.'

'Treat yourself to one, then, while you get us another round,' I instruct her with a wink.

'That's very kind of you, sir,' she says charmingly, 'but I can't drink on duty.'

'Well, then you'll just have to have a drink with us when

you're off duty instead,' I flirt, pleased at the low ripple of admiration that I sense from the other men at our table. But even better is the knowing smile Stephanie gives me as she turns to leave.

I feel fantastic.

Why can't I feel like this all the time? Actually I know why. It's because I have a stressful job that requires me to spend twelve hours a day in an office, and when I get home, I have two noisy kids to try to control as well as a wife who loves me but hardly excites me. But, tonight, I am having fun, and I don't intend to bring it to a halt anytime soon.

I spend the rest of the evening flirting with Stephanie while keeping up a flow of very generous tips until I'm certain that she is smitten with me. By the time this bar is closing, I'm pretty sure she'll be receptive to my offer of the two of us going elsewhere for a drink before we call it a night.

After calling them a taxi and telling them we'll have to do this again soon, I manage to successfully lose my companions. I wait for Stephanie to finish before inviting her for a cocktail at a bar that I know stays open late. But we barely even make it in there before Stephanie asks me how far away my place is, and once I've called my own taxi, we're on our way there, or at least we're on our way to the place I call my second home.

As the taxi pulls up, I look at the property's dark windows and think about how this is the first time I've been back here since I watched David's body being carried out of the front door in a crate. That might mean that going inside could feel a little uncomfortable, but I try not to worry too much about that and focus instead on the young waitress beside me. She seems a little surprised when she realises that this is my house, probably having assumed I'd be living somewhere more extravagant, but I tell her this is just one of my many properties as I pay the driver and lead her inside.

The house is cold, but I sense I'll soon be warmed up, and as Stephanie puts her lips to mine, the chilly conditions begin to thaw out. We keep kissing as we make our way rather awkwardly to the staircase, our passion getting in the way of the practicality of watching where we are going, so we both stumble and fall onto the carpet. Stephanie doesn't seem to mind and is eager to carry on with what we've started. I'm returning her ardour and starting to wonder if we'll even make it up to the bedroom.

Until I realise where we are lying.

This is the same spot of carpet.

It's where I killed David.

This is exactly where his body lay after I pushed him down the stairs and stamped on his face, his chest, his flanks. And now, instead of looking down and seeing a beautiful young woman beneath me, I only see one thing.

David and his lifeless eyes.

'You okay?' Stephanie asks, no doubt wondering what she might have done wrong for me to want to stop kissing her.

'Oh, yeah. More than okay,' I reply, and I force myself to try to carry on. But no matter how much I try, being in this part of the house is preventing me from focusing on anything other than the man I killed, so I suggest we take things to the bedroom. Stephanie has no problem with that, so we move on upstairs, and as we do, I hope what just happened there was a blip rather than an indication of something that is going to cause me problems in the future.

The last thing I want is to be tormented by thoughts of David every time I bring somebody back here. This place was always supposed to be my sanctuary, an escape from my real life, a house where I could be the old me rather than the husband and daddy that I'm obliged to be in my other house. But maybe it won't be that easy. Maybe I'll have to sell this place and find somewhere new. I'll see how things go. But right now, we're in the bedroom, and David is slipping from my mind as I watch Stephanie slip out of that sexy waitress uniform of hers.

It's late, and I'll have to be home in an hour or so. Staying out much later will only make Maria suspicious. But that still gives me sixty minutes to enjoy myself.

And enjoy myself I will.

29

MARIA

William had a late night last night 'entertaining clients', as he puts it on his expense returns when he files them with accounts. But now it's time for me to have a little 'extracurricular' activity of my own outside the office, and unlike him, I'm doing it during the day.

I've told him I've gone to meet a friend for lunch, giving myself an excuse to escape the office. William didn't object to that plan, telling me to enjoy myself before the big meetings start tomorrow. But I'm not meeting a friend for lunch. Instead, I'm going across town to the office where our former HR manager is now employed. I'm on my way to see Becky. I'm just praying that she can enlighten me a little more about what's been going on at my company, specifically those activities that my husband has been working so hard to keep under wraps.

The office I have come to is not quite as big or as lavishly decorated as the one I work in; it's clear this is a smaller place for a smaller business. But maybe that's what drew Becky here. Maybe she liked the thought of working in a smaller team. I might ask her if that's the case. But first, I need to ask the receptionist if Becky can actually see me now.

I wait patiently as she makes a call while doing my best to look friendly and reinforce what I just said, which is that I'm an old friend and colleague of Becky's, and I'd love to see her for a quick catch-up while I'm passing. But, unfortunately, the receptionist tells me that Becky isn't answering her phone, so it seems like I might have had a wasted journey.

Frustrated, but doing my best not to show it, I thank the receptionist and go to leave, figuring I'll have to come back here some other time. But then I walk through the exit, and as I do, I see the person I wanted to talk to coming right towards me with a packaged sandwich and a bottle of juice in her hand.

It looks like Becky went out to get her lunch.

And it also looks like she is shocked to see me.

'Maria? What are you doing here?' she asks, almost dropping her supplies.

'Hello, Becky!' I greet her warmly as if this were a perfectly normal encounter. 'I've just popped in to see you.'

'Me? Why?'

'Well, to be honest, I was hoping we could have a quick chat. There's a few things I really like to ask you, if you've got a moment, please.'

Becky glances around nervously.

'Please. Just five minutes,' I say. 'Then I'll leave you to enjoy your lunch.'

Becky looks very unsure, but then concedes, and I suggest we take a seat together on one of the benches on the grassy, landscaped area outside her workplace. Once there, I get right into it.

'How's the new job going?' I ask. 'Well, I hope?'

'It's okay.'

'Oh, good.' I guess I'll have to work quite hard here if she's going to speak freely with me. 'Do you enjoy it more than – well, than your last one?'

'It's different,' Becky says, still looking very nervous. 'Look, Maria, why are you here?'

'I wanted to talk to you about Adelina.'

Becky almost recoils from me at the sound of her name, turns the bottle of juice anxiously over in her hands. 'What about her?'

'I've found out that my husband gave her money around the time of her harassment claim and just before she left my company. Do you know anything about that?'

'No, I don't,' Becky replies, and I think she is telling the truth.

'Fair enough, thank you.' I turn slightly to meet her eye. 'But you obviously know about the money my husband gave you just after you left, right?'

Becky doesn't say anything there, so I carry on.

'Five grand, wasn't it? Can you tell me what that was for?'

'I'm not sure.'

'You're not sure?'

'No.' She shakes her head, and I sense her embarrassment and fear. 'He just gave it to me. I didn't ask for it. I didn't even know I was going to get it. I'd already worked my last day. Then I saw it go into my account.'

'Didn't you think to find out what it was for?'

'No.'

'Why, Becky? If somebody put a big chunk of money into my account, then I'd want to know why.'

Becky shrugs as if to dismiss my questions, but I have the feeling she is keeping something from me.

'Did it have anything to do with Adelina and the harassment claim?'

'What?' she protests. 'I don't know what you're talking about.'

'Really? So the money wasn't connected with the investigation – *your* investigation, in fact – that found David guilty?'

'Look, Maria. I'm sorry, I can't help you. I don't work for you anymore, so I'm going to go now.'

Becky stands to leave, but I grab her arm, not in a forceful way but more out of desperation. It feels like I'm not getting anywhere with this. Whatever my husband might have done – and why – is still a total mystery to me.

'William has been lying to me,' I confess. 'He didn't tell me about the payment to Adelina, and when I asked if there were any others I didn't know about, he told me there weren't. But then I found the one to you, so I know something is going on here. I just don't know what it is. That's why I'm here. I'm hoping you can help me.'

'I'm sorry, Maria, but I can't.'

Becky releases herself from my grip, and I realise I'm going to lose any chance I have of getting her to talk unless I do something drastic. Unless I break promises, the way William has broken his to me.

'David came to my house,' I tell her before she can escape. 'He threatened me with a knife.'

'What?' Becky cries, sitting back down next to me in shock. 'A knife? David?'

'He broke in and held a knife to my throat, Becky. William was there too. I thought he was going to kill us.'

'Oh my God! Why would he do that?'

'He was angry about what happened with Adelina,' I explain. 'He insisted he was innocent and blamed us for not investigating it properly. I thought he was crazy, but then I found out about the money to Adelina, and now I'm not so sure. I think William is hiding something from me. And I think you might know what it is.'

'I'm sorry,' she says, back on the defensive. 'But I don't know what it is.'

'Come on, Becky. You can tell me. You don't have to be afraid of him. He'll never know that I talked to you. Please just tell me what you know about that harassment case – I thought I knew everything, but clearly not.'

Becky's eyes remain fearful, but I'm not too proud to keep begging her until she gives me something. Which, eventually, she does.

'Look, all I know is William was very keen to keep it quiet. He was happy for us to find David guilty and get rid of him quickly, even though I argued that we should at least give him the chance to defend himself. But William wanted him gone.'

'So, could he have been innocent?'

'I don't know. Maybe.'

'Is that why you left? You felt guilty?'

Becky doesn't say anything, so I take that as a yes.

'And that's why he gave you money. As a way to buy your silence? To stop you reporting any irregular practices at Gallagher's.'

'I guess. But I wouldn't have done it anyway. I was as much to blame as him. I was the HR manager. I had a professional duty to act in accordance with the book, and I didn't. I let William dictate what happened when I should have been impartial.'

'Why didn't you stand up to him? Why didn't you insist on a proper investigation if you knew it was wrong to assume David's guilt?'

'I don't know. I let myself down. I guess I was afraid.'

'Afraid of William?'

'Yes.' She looks utterly downcast. 'He was the boss. I had to do what he said.'

'I'm the boss too. You could have spoken to me.'

'I know. Maria, I'm sorry.'

I can see how distressed Becky is about this, and it pains me to realise that she was most likely at least this distressed when she worked for us, which is why she resigned. But I didn't notice; I stupidly assumed she was leaving to progress her career, not because my husband had – at best – made her feel uncomfortable.

'I'm sorry too, Becky.' I feel I should go now before I upset her further. But I still need to ask one more question. 'Do you have any idea where Adelina might be?'

'No. None.'

'Are you sure, Becky? To be honest, I'm worried about her.'

'Look, I've told you all I know. I really need to go now.'

Becky glances back at her office, and I nod to let her know that she's free to leave. As I watch her hurry inside her new workplace, I feel a little envious.

She gets to have a fresh start, whereas I have to go back to that other office.

The one that's harbouring secrets.

The one where William has done all manner of illicit things.

WILLIAM

I've played all sorts of roles recently. Boss. Husband. Lover.

Murderer.

But now it's time to focus on one role I might have been neglecting a little, and that's the role of daddy.

I'm sitting on the floor of our playroom, the one that is stuffed full of all sorts of games, toys and other noisy things that give me a headache. Edward and Penny are in here with me, and the two of them are competing for my attention by each playing with whatever thing interests them the most. Unfortunately, those things are different, and despite my insistence that it would be much easier for the three of us to play together if we just settled on one thing, neither of my children wants to hear it.

Edward is desperate to play some kind of football game, and he has set out all the little figurines on a big green mat that is supposed to represent the pitch, while Penny has a very intricate dolls house full of all sorts of miniature characters, not to mention furniture, and she is telling me where to be move all these tiny items between each room.

I barely remember buying any of this stuff, but then that's hardly a surprise because Maria tends to deal with birthdays and Christmas. I just watch the kids open their respective presents and nod along once each one is revealed, as if I knew what was hidden within the wrapping paper all along. But I can't be expected to keep track of everything my children have in this house. I can barely keep track of my own stuff, I think, and that's when I remember that I've accidentally left my briefcase in the car again.

I instruct Edward and Penny to play nicely together for a moment while I go out to my car and collect the briefcase from the back seat. But, as I tell myself when I leave the play-room, I make sure not to indulge in any flashbacks that occur as I revisit that place where so many awful things happened.

I'm absolutely not going to dwell on the memory of being handcuffed on this back seat while my wife was imprisoned against her will, just like I absolutely refuse to dwell on the fact that I almost lost my mojo with that waitress the other night as we rolled around on the floor near to where David lost his life.

I'm not going to be one of those people who falls apart because they are haunted by their past. I'm stronger than that, and I've proven it already by how far I've come and all I've accomplished since those terrible things happened. It's true that I killed Adelina months ago, but my professional performance has never been better, and the unfortunate David incident aside, my home life is honestly great too. That tells me that what happened with David will gradually fade away into the background just like what happened with Adelina did. That's a comforting thought and certainly one that's more comforting than the alternative, which is allowing myself to be tormented by any trauma.

Unfortunately, I'm not sure my wife is as strong as I am.

As I re-enter the house, I hear my wife cry out in pain in the kitchen. I drop my briefcase, and I run in to see her running her hand under the cold tap. It's pretty obvious that she just burnt herself on the hob while preparing dinner.

'Are you okay?' I ask, but she just shakes her head, and I fear that her troubles are not limited to kitchen mishaps. She's distracted, not quite herself. Basically, she still hasn't gotten over what she went through with David.

'Come on, you sit down, and I'll finish dinner,' I say, but she shakes her head again and mutters something about how she'll be fine in a minute.

But then I see something that proves she knows it's all a lie.

Tears.

My wife is crying.

And I'm not sure what I can say to make it better.

'What's the matter?' I ask once the tap has been turned off. 'Talk to me. Please.'

'I told you, I'm fine,' Maria replies, wiping her eyes and returning to the pan of food bubbling away.

'Maybe you need to talk to somebody,' I suggest gently. 'You know, about what happened.'

'I can't, can I? You said we mustn't tell anybody.'

'You wouldn't give them David's name, of course. And anything else you told them would be between patient and professional. They'd be obliged to maintain confidentiality.'

'William, I don't need a therapist.'

'You need something, my love. You're crying in our kitchen, and not just because you've burnt yourself.'

'I'm fine! Just leave me alone!'

I'm stunned at Maria's outburst, and she even looks a little shocked herself. But Edward and Penny are shocked the most as the pair of them timidly enter the kitchen to see what's going on between their parents.

I recite Maria's oft-repeated line that their mummy is fine before I usher the two little ones out and give my wife some privacy. I try to distract myself by returning to the games I was playing with the kids, but it's impossible to concentrate. All this time I've been so focused on myself and making sure that I was covering my tracks and keeping my head in the game that I've lost sight of making sure my own wife is okay.

I was serious when I suggested the therapist. It could do her good. If not, then maybe a holiday is in order. A couple of weeks away. The four of us. Get some sun. Forget about work. Let somebody else cover for us while we relax and unwind. I'll suggest that to Maria later, once the kids are in bed, if she still isn't keen on the therapist idea. Hopefully the scene in the kitchen was just a blip, and it won't turn into a bigger problem. But that remains to be seen.

Dinner passes by uneventfully, which I'm very grateful for, and as I clear the dishes away, Maria takes the kids upstairs to get them ready for bed. I stifle a couple of yawns as I work. I've always found domestic life dull.

Dishwasher duty. Dustbin duty. Random toys away in the basket duty. Yawn.

Death sometimes seems more exciting than that. But I do what I can to help around the house, and once the kitchen is clean again, I join the rest of my family upstairs.

'Read me a story, Daddy!' Penny cries when she sees me enter her bedroom, so I wink at Maria before doing just that.

It takes three stories before my daughter drifts off, and I add a silent prayer to those as I leave her room, hoping she has an undisturbed night's sleep without any bad dreams to stir her from her slumber.

Edward is flicking through one of his favourite football

magazines when I go in to see him, and we spend a bit of time talking about this player and that before I tell him to get some rest. He has a big match coming up at school at the end of the week, and he won't score any goals if he's tired. I've found that making my son fear a bad performance on the football pitch is the best way to get him to turn off his bedside light and put his head on his pillow at a decent hour. It works again now as he rolls over and says a sleepy goodnight.

Okay, that's the kids taken care of.

Now it's on to my wife.

I must have been longer than I thought with the children, because I find Maria in our bedroom undressing for her own bedtime. I approach her for a hug, although I'm a little tentative after her sharp words earlier. It seems I'm not the only one. Maria flinches at my touch.

'Hey, what's wrong?' I ask. She's never reacted like that to me in all the time we've been together.

But then she says those two words again, the words that make me want to scream.

'I'm fine.'

I leave her while I get myself ready for bed, and even though it's early, I think it's clear that we might as well call it a night because neither of us seems to be in the mood for television, conversation or anything else.

With the lights off, I stare up at the ceiling, wishing I knew what was going on in my wife's head. But then she asks me a question that gives me more of a clue than I might like.

'Adelina was the only bonus you kept secret from me, right?'

That question unnerves me and not just because I know I have to lie to answer it. It's because it tells me Maria is clearly still thinking about that time she knows I lied to her, and that means she's probably wondering what else there might be.

'You already asked me that question,' I remind her.

'And you told me there was nothing else.'

'Yes,' I confirm. After all, that is what I told her, so I'd better stick to my story.

'Okay. Goodnight, William.'

She rolls over then, and that seems to be it. But I can't sleep now. Not after that.

I wait for what seems like an age until I'm sure that Maria is asleep before I reach out for my mobile and type an email to our IT manager, Sarah. I mention that I'll need her to look at something for me in the office tomorrow and let her know I'll come and see her as soon as I get in. Then I put my phone down and try to get some rest. But it's not easy. Not now I feel sure I need to have somebody search through what my wife has been looking at on the company server.

Has she been looking for another example of when I might have lied to her?

Has she been analysing old transactions?

And if so, has she spotted the strictly unofficial bonus I gave to Becky?

I guess I'll find out tomorrow.

Until then, I won't know for sure if my wife knows I'm still lying to her.

I also won't know what her next move might be.

31

MARIA

I didn't sleep last night. I'm sure William thought I did because I was so still beside him, but I was awake the whole time. I saw the light go on from his phone at one point, and I guess he couldn't sleep either. That's hardly a surprise considering the atmosphere that exists between the pair of us at the moment.

Things aren't great.

I lost my cool with my husband yesterday after burning my hand thanks to being so distracted. I refused to tell William what the real issue is, though, insisting that I was fine, although he knows me better than that. I did give him a hint later on by asking if there had been any more pay-outs that I didn't know about, which was also his final chance to tell me the truth. Sadly for me, and potentially our marriage, he chose to lie again, and that means he's out of chances now. If he'd just admitted he'd given Becky money, then things might have been okay. He might have even given me a perfectly reasonable explanation as to why he'd done it and why he'd kept it from me. But his lies can only mean that he is hiding something.

His lies mean he is lacking something that all good relationships need.

Respect for the other person.

How can he respect me when he keeps deceiving me? That's not how a person should treat anybody, let alone their wife.

I kept things civil this morning as we woke up and got ourselves and the kids ready for the day ahead. He might be thinking that whatever was wrong with me yesterday is a thing of the past and that I'm doing much better after a proper night's rest. But he would be wrong there. If anything, I'm even angrier at him, not to mention more determined to find out the truth. That's why I've come to a fairly dramatic decision.

I'm going to contact somebody who could help give me some of the answers I'm desperately seeking about my husband.

But, honestly, how does one go about hiring a private investigator? I've seen a few TV shows where a character finds a business card in a phone box on a misty street corner and calls the number to summon some shady figure in a trench coat who likes to lurk in bushes clutching a Polaroid camera. But I've assumed there are easier ways to go about it in the modern age, so I've turned to the internet.

I'm sitting in the office with William only a few feet away, oblivious as to what I am doing as I browse the internet on my phone to find somebody who can – what? – start following him ... He's typing away on his laptop, muttering something about some stupid client who doesn't read their emails properly. While he's doing that, I browse the websites that my search has generated, and as I do, I realise it's not going to be that difficult to find the kind of person I need. There are plenty of people advertising their services, which range from investigating somebody in a very specific way all the way up to keeping surveillance on them for twenty-four hours a day, seven days a week.

I imagine that latter option is a very expensive one, but what if it's the one I need? What if it's the only way I'll ever truly know what my husband is up to? But maybe a forensic search of his electronic devices would start to yield some answers. His mobile. The laptop in his home study. Would they be the best places to start?

Would they hold some answers to the mystery of Adelina, David and Becky?

I have plenty to ponder as the day wears on, not least of which is choosing which PI to contact. It's usually best to get at least a couple of quotes when requiring a contractor to carry out a service, but does such protocol apply to something like this? Or does one simply ring a PI, give them the target and ask them to report back when they have something?

I don't know. This isn't something I ever thought I'd have to do. I certainly didn't think I'd be so paranoid about my husband while I was standing next to him at the altar on our wedding day. But here we are. Life is unpredictable, and I should know that better than anyone by now. I can almost still feel the touch of that blade on my neck if I close my eyes and focus on it, just like I can feel the hurt when William lied to me in bed last night.

None of that is going away, at least not until I do something about it.

William leaves the office to attend a meeting with a couple of the guys from the sales team who he feels need a bit of a pep talk to improve their paltry figures, so I smile at him as he leaves the room. Then I pick up my phone and take another look at my list of options.

I'll just have to pick one.

Hope they are good.

Hope they know what they're doing.

Most of all, I'll have to hope William won't have any idea that I've hired a PI to watch him.

32

WILLIAM

I've told my wife that I'm going into a meeting with my sales team to encourage them to improve their productivity, but, as is becoming commonplace, it was a barefaced lie. Instead, I've come to meet Sarah, who should have that report I asked of her ready for me by now.

Sure enough, she has done what has been required, and as I take a seat opposite her, she hands me the report.

'This is everything my wife has been looking at on the server recently?' I double-check as my eyes scan the lines of text on the piece of paper.

'Yes.' Sarah nods, but her answer is quiet, and she looks very unsure. If I had to guess, I'd say she feels uncomfortable with handling such a request. I can see why it might seem a little odd for one owner of the company to want to know what the other owner has been doing at work. Even more so when those owners are married. But Sarah doesn't have to concern herself with such qualms. She just needs to do whatever I ask of her while she's in my employment.

I see lots of things on this report that don't look out of the ordinary, which is a relief, allowing me to skim through this data quickly. What I'm looking for specifically is any evidence that Maria has been looking into areas she wouldn't usually access.

Like the accounts, for example.

But that's exactly what she has done.

I grit my teeth as I see how she has trawled through our main account's history all the way back to a certain date. *The time of Adelina's bonus.* And because she's gone back that far, I know she will have seen something else. The money I gave to Becky after she left. And there it is, right in the middle of the page, the keystrokes that Maria made now printed in black and white. My wife has seen that payment to Becky, and that's how she'll know I lied again.

Damn it.

That must be why she asked me about it in bed last night. It was a test.

And I failed it.

Why did I give Becky that money? She'd already moved on from the company; I should have just left it. But I didn't. I thought I could guarantee she would look back on her time working for me more fondly if she received a surprise payment after she left rather than having her worry about how we had more than likely dismissed somebody who hadn't been proven of guilty of sexual harassment.

'Is everything okay?' Sarah asks, and her question reminds me that I'm still sitting in her office. I'd almost forgotten she was here, such was my level of distraction.

'Yeah, fine,' I mutter. I put the report down after once again satisfying myself that I've now seen everything Maria has seen too.

'It's just, well, I thought it was quite an unusual request,' Sarah goes on. 'I was worried something might have happened. Between you and Maria, I mean.'

'Oh no. Please don't worry about it,' I say as graciously as I can, but I'm barely even focusing on Sarah. My mind is already whirring away as I try to figure out what to do next.

If my wife already knows I'm lying to her, then why hasn't she confronted me? Why is she playing games with me? What else could she possibly be doing?

I need to know, and I need to know now, so with that in mind, I have another assignment for my intrepid IT manager.

'This has been very useful,' I tell Sarah. 'Thank you. But now I need you to create a report of what my wife has been looking at on her company mobile.' I know now what Maria has been searching for on her laptop, but I suspect her phone hides even more things, things that might give me some idea as to what she is planning to do next. For all I know, she might be reading forums about wives who can't trust their husbands. She might be googling divorce lawyers. But, worst of all, she might be reading about what to do if you suspect your partner of being a criminal.

'Her company mobile?' Sarah repeats, and I can tell she's seriously uncomfortable with such a request. 'Why?'

'Because I've asked you to.'

It's a stern reply, but I'm hoping it's all I need to get Sarah to comply.

Maria's work mobile is the only device she really uses. We tell staff to use their own personal phones when they're not on company time, but, in practice, most people don't, and Maria and I are included in that number. And now this is working in my favour.

But Sarah is still not convinced.

'I'm sorry. I'm not sure I can do that. I mean, the most

straightforward way to do this would be for me to have her actual phone ...'

'That's fine. Just tell her it needs a software update and take it for a couple of hours. She'll never know, not if you tell her everyone else's phone requires the same thing.'

That will work, but Sarah still has a problem.

'I'm sorry. I'm really not comfortable about this. If this is about something going on between you and your wife, then I don't want to get involved.'

I realise then that I'm going to have to be a little craftier than simply giving her orders to follow. I need to be clever. I need to do what I always do.

I need to lie.

'You're right. I'm sorry,' I begin, holding my hands up. 'I can see how this might appear to be a weird thing for me to ask. It's just ...'

I deliberately allow my voice to trail off until Sarah asks me what is wrong.

'It's just that I'm worried my wife might be having an affair,' I confess, avoiding eye contact so that I look as shameful about this as possible.

'What? Maria? You're joking?'

I shake my head to show that this is a very serious matter.

'Oh, William! I'm so sorry. What's happened?'

I look up at Sarah then with an expression that says 'Don't ask', and she quickly apologises for prying.

'I'm sorry for even asking you,' I say, laying it on thick. 'And I'm sorry if it makes you uncomfortable. You don't have to do it if you don't want to. Please just forget about it. I'm sure everything will be fine.'

I'm hoping that my acting skills are up to par; I'm praying Sarah will fall for them hook, line and sinker.

And she does. She takes pity on me. She tells me she will do as I ask.

'Thank you,' I say, putting on an expression suited to the troubled husband who might be having his heart broken. 'I really appreciate it.'

I go to leave Sarah's office then, satisfied that the next part of my plan to find out what my wife is up to has been set in motion, but my IT manager has one more thing to say.

'If you need to talk,' she tells me, 'I'm here.'

'Thank you,' I reply. 'That's really kind.'

We share a small smile before I leave. But my face drops once I'm out of sight, and that's because I'm now on my way back to the office I share with my wife.

But I'll just have to put on another fake smile when I get there.

And I'll keep up that fake smile for as long as I have to until I know for sure that Maria isn't going to find out anything else about me that she shouldn't.

33

MARIA

William came back from his meeting and with the news that everything had gone well, although I wasn't quite convinced given how quiet he was for the next few hours. He's barely said a word to me all morning, and it's actually a bit of a relief when the tension in our office is broken by the appearance of Sarah, who has something she needs to ask me.

'Hey. I'm really sorry for the inconvenience, but I'm just doing a quick software update on everyone's phones, and I'm afraid it's your turn,' she says as she reaches my desk.

'Oh, okay,' I reply, reaching for my handbag so I can take out my phone. 'Do you need to take it away, or can you do it here?'

'I'm afraid I'll have to take it away. But I'll bring it back as soon as I can.'

I shrug. This is a bit annoying, but I do as she asks because who am I to question her superior IT wisdom?

I hand her my phone, and she thanks me before going to leave.

'Don't you need William's as well?' I ask as she reaches the door, and she turns back and looks across at my husband.

'Oh, erm,' Sarah says, seemingly confused. 'I thought it best if I didn't take both of yours at once. In case you got an important call or something.'

'That's thoughtful of you, Sarah, but don't worry about it; you can do mine as well,' William says, and he holds up his phone.

She scurries to his desk and accepts it before leaving the room in a rush.

I have a midday meeting to get to, so I make a move for that a moment later, wishing I still had my phone with me and hoping it will be ready once I come out of this and go for my lunch. But when I take my seat in the meeting room and jokingly mention to a few colleagues about how I feel naked without my phone, I'm met by some blank faces.

It seems that nobody else has been asked to hand theirs in for a software update.

'Just one minute,' I say as I excuse myself from the room. Before I know it, I'm on my way to see Sarah, and I'm almost bubbling over with paranoia about what might have been really going on during that awkward encounter in our office earlier.

Maybe it's okay. Maybe there's nothing weird about her asking me for my phone.

After all, William handed his over as well.

Or at least he did so voluntarily, without actually being asked for it, which might have been a way to make the whole thing seem less weird.

I knock on Sarah's door, and when I enter, I see my phone

connected to a cable that runs into her laptop. I can't see what's on her screen, but it's obvious she must be working on something.

'Maria?' She jumps, startled when she sees me. 'Is everything okay?'

'Yeah, I'm sorry. I just need my phone back.'

'Oh, I've not quite finished updating it yet.'

'That's okay, I'll give it back later. You can do everybody else's while you're waiting.'

I hold out my hand, but she hesitates.

'Sarah, give me my phone.'

My stern instruction achieves the compliance I require. That's one good thing about being in charge here. My employees do what I tell them.

'But I was just wondering, why did you ask for my phone and nobody else's?' I ask, studying Sarah's face for signs of nervousness as she considers her answer.

'Oh, no reason. I just like to start at the top and work my way down,' she says, but I don't buy it.

'Sarah, is there something you're not telling me?'

'No, not at all.'

'You're lying.'

Sarah is blushing now. She really is a bad liar. And right now, I'm in a really bad mood. I say nothing, simply hold her gaze.

'It's nothing,' she maintains, but she's cracking.

'Sarah ...'

I eyeball her until she concedes.

'William asked me to look at your phone.'

'What? Why?'

Sarah shrugs, and I'm about to storm out of the room and go confront my husband when she speaks again.

'He's a good man. He loves you. I just think he's worried.'

'Worried? About what?'

'About getting hurt.'

'Hurt? What's that supposed to mean?'

I wait for Sarah to answer me, but she doesn't, so I ask her again. And then she says it.

She says the most ridiculous thing I've ever heard.

'He thinks you might be having an affair.'

It's a good job I'm not susceptible to swooning and fainting because if I were, then I would probably drop to the floor after hearing such a thing. What utter nonsense. Why would William say something so stupid and untrue? But then, I remind myself, my husband doesn't do anything without thinking it through, so he must have had a good reason. I'm guessing Sarah wasn't entirely comfortable snooping through my phone, so he made up some crazy excuse as to why it had to be done. He was trying to garner her sympathy. But he's gone too far this time.

Or has he?

Taking a moment to consider my options, I realise that calling William out on this will only alert him to the fact that I've rumbled him. But if I just give my phone back and let Sarah conduct her search, he won't know that I'm still one step ahead of him.

'Look, Sarah, I can assure you I'm not cheating on my husband,' I tell her. 'To prove it, I'll happily hand my phone back over. But you mustn't tell William that we had this conversation, okay? Let him think that I still have no idea what you are doing. All right?'

Sarah nods.

'Good. Okay, I just need to check my calendar for this afternoon; then you can have my phone for as long as you want. Deal?'

Sarah nods again, and I waste no time in going straight onto the internet to conduct a couple of searches for my husband to see. If he's looking for something that might worry him, then I'm going to make damn sure that he finds it.

It takes me less than a minute to do what I need to do, and then I hand my phone over to Sarah with a reminder to keep quiet about our little conversation. Then I return to my meeting, but I don't hear a single word that's said. I'm too busy thinking about William and how he will react when he receives that report from Sarah.

She's going to have uncovered a few troubling things.

And once he sees what they are, he's going to find it very difficult to keep playing it cool.

34

WILLIAM

I saw Sarah enter my office and hand my wife her mobile back half an hour ago, so in order not to arouse suspicion, I've waited patiently for a little while before going to see my IT manager and asking for everything she found on the phone. When I do, Sarah seems uneasy with me, but I remind her again that she is doing me a favour and that I wouldn't be asking her to help me if I didn't think there might be something amiss with my wife.

After she's sent me the digital file of what she took from Maria's mobile, I take my laptop to an empty meeting room and sit down to pore over it. There's all sorts in this folder. There's photos my wife has taken, including some of the kids, and while not using company phones for personal images was another rule we made when we drew up this company's staff handbook, it's yet another rule that those in management like to bend and break a little.

I check the text messages and emails, but there's nothing of interest. Just boring business stuff, as it should be. Then I come to the final part of this folder, the part that lists my wife's entire internet search history. It's lengthy, as I expected it to be considering she has been in possession of that particular phone for at least two years, so I waste no time in skimming through it.

There are searches that relate to issues in our industry. There are links to videos that teach the viewer how to become more efficient in the workplace. And there are a few personal searches like 'Best places to go on holiday in November' or 'Birthday gifts for seven-year-olds'. But then I see something a little more concerning. It's a search my wife made today.

She's been googling 'Discreet local private investigators'.

I try to keep calm as I run through possible reasons why Maria might have been searching for such a thing. But it's hard when I can come to only one conclusion.

She is looking for somebody to investigate me.

While it's incredibly galling to learn that my wife wants to hire a third party to find out as much as they can about me, I am at least glad that I've discovered this before she's had time to hire somebody. That allows me the opportunity to curtail all the behaviours that could land me in trouble with her, namely meeting women in bars and taking them back to Sharples Road, but it also gives me the chance to make sure I don't do anything that could land me in trouble with the police.

Thank God I wasn't being watched when I killed Adelina and David. If I had been, then I certainly wouldn't be sitting in this plush, air-conditioned office right now wearing a £1,000 bespoke suit and working on a brand-new laptop. I'd be wearing prison clothes and sharing a concrete cell with somebody I probably would prefer not to be in the company of.

Enlightened about my wife's interest in a PI, I carry on looking through the various internet links Maria has clicked on, as well as some of her search terms.

And then I get another shock.

Despite the cool temperature in this room, I feel beads of sweat forming on my forehead as I read the terrifying items my wife has searched for as recently as today.

What to do if your husband is lying to you

What to do if you think your husband is keeping secrets

But worst of all ...

How to report your husband to the police.

I lean back from the laptop, as if distancing myself from what I have just read on the screen will help matters. But of course it doesn't. My paranoia has gone into overdrive.

It's obvious that Maria is on to me. She knows about the secret bonuses, but what else does she know? Who has she spoken to? What has she seen? Does she know that I'm so much more than a liar?

Does she know that I have killed people?

I want to go and ask her. No, scratch that. I *need* to go and ask her. I have to know everything she knows and, if this is as bad as I think it is, I need to convince her that she doesn't have to involve anybody else, most of all the police. I'm still the man she fell in love with. I'm still the father of her kids.

She won't ruin me, will she?

Can I afford to take the risk of finding out?

I can't give Maria the chance to raise any suspicions or

accusations against me. The thought of being questioned by the police over any of this, whether it's the harassment claim or Adelina and David, is just unbearable. I know I'd struggle to keep my cool during the interrogation. I'd slip up. Make a mistake. And then all my crimes would come tumbling out.

But it's not just me I'm thinking about. It's this company too. Imagine the reputational damage it would suffer if one of its owners was found to have committed such serious crimes. A war between me and Maria would tear this company apart and leave me ruined financially, although the loss of my freedom would override that terrifying fate.

What should I do? Confront my wife before she takes this any further? Try to convince her that I'm innocent and, if that doesn't work, try to convince her that it would be better for her if she kept quiet? Or should I just take the initiative? Do what I'm already thinking about doing so that this doesn't get any worse than it already is?

Should I simply silence her permanently?

I leave the office without saying a word to anybody and go straight home, arriving in my study less than twenty minutes after I left that air-conditioned meeting room where I learnt of my wife's internet searches. Once I'm seated in front of my personal laptop, I access the dark web again, a place I'd hoped never to go back to but a place that is always there, existing for people like me, people who are willing to seek out those things that would disgust the average, respectable citizen.

It doesn't take me long to find the contact information for the man I'm looking for. It's the man I have used before. A man who did a very good job the last time I hired him.

He's a professional.

I type out a quick message before hesitating over the Send icon.

If I do this, life will never be the same again. For me. For my kids. And, most of all, for my wife.

But I can't see any other choice. I have to stop Maria from learning more about my past. I have to stop her before she gets the police involved.

I have to have her killed.

'I've got another job for you,' the message on my screen reads.

And now it's gone. Now it will already be in the inbox of the man with the plastic sheeting and the crate and the saw. And perhaps he will already be wondering who the next body he needs to dispose of belongs to.

As if he was waiting by his own computer for such a message to appear, he responds quickly, telling me he is available and that the fee will be the same as last time. The money isn't a problem. What will be a problem is actually creating the body for this man to dispose of in the first place. How will I kill Maria? Smother her? Strangle her? Stab her? Every way I can think of seems so brutal. At least it was a little easier with Adelina and David; I had no emotional attachment to those two. But we're talking about the mother of my children here.

This is very, very different.

That's why I need an easier method of taking a life than doing it by brute force. Preferably, I need to do it without even having to put my hands on her.

And then I think of it. The thing I used to joke about all the time. The way I would jest with friends at dinner parties about how I always knew the perfect method for killing my wife. All I had to do was give her a very specific sort of food.

Food that she's allergic to.

Peanuts.

That's how I'll do it. I'll sprinkle some in her dinner.

Better yet, I'll get someone else to do it for me. The further this is from me, the better.

If I do it this way, I won't have to go through a whole charade of reporting my wife missing and becoming a suspect while her disappearance is investigated. Everybody will know exactly what happened to her.

She will have died of anaphylactic shock.

It will be a tragedy. I'll get so much sympathy. But I won't get in any trouble. I'll get away with it again, like I have always done so far.

I reply to the email I just received, sending more correspondence across the murk of the dark web to the man waiting to hear from me. But I've had to disappoint him. I've told him that there has been a change of plan and that his services are no longer required.

He doesn't reply to that, but it doesn't matter now because I don't need him.

All I need is a delivery driver to bring some food to my house tonight for my wife to enjoy.

Food that will be the last meal she ever eats.

35

MARIA

There's a lot going on with me right now. But the same can be said for my husband, who rather mysteriously left the office for a little while this afternoon. When he reappeared, he was holding a bunch of flowers and a box of chocolates, and he presented them to me in our office, no doubt after attracting the curious glances of several of our colleagues who must have seen him walk through the office with such obviously romantic gifts.

'What are these for?' I asked him as I accepted them.

'I know that things haven't been great between us recently,' he replied. 'But I just wanted to remind you that I love you.'

Under different circumstances, such a gesture would have tugged on my heartstrings and made me feel like I was the luckiest woman in the world to be married to such a caring man. But considering everything that's been going on, it took all my effort to smile weakly and force out a 'thank you' before I put the flowers and chocolates down and let him go on.

'I was thinking ... How about we have another night to ourselves. Pack the kids off to your parents again. Try to have the romantic evening we were denied last time.'

'Are you sure?'

'Yeah, I was thinking we could get a takeaway. Maybe from that great Indian restaurant on the high street. We haven't had one for a while, have we? Do you want to check with your parents and see if they'll have the kids?'

Wow, he's got it all worked out ...

My mind was ablaze with thoughts of what my husband might be up to. But I was also enticed by the strong possibility that those decoy internet searches that I purposefully made on my phone had forced him into doing something a little different.

'Yeah, sounds good,' I told him, and that was that. A date night was set. The two of us were going to be alone in the house together. The last time we tried that, a man broke in and tried to kill me.

Now I fear that the danger might already be inside my home.

I left the office before William, telling him I'd pick the kids up from school and drop them at my parents' house while he finished up at work. He told me he'd order the take-away before he left and asked me for my order, which I told him was my usual one.

After collecting Edward and Penny and giving them the exciting news that they were going for a sleepover at their grandparents' house again, I helped them pack a few things before taking them around to my mum and dad. I made sure to give each of my parents a hug when I saw them, before giving even bigger hugs to my two little ones, squeezing their bodies tightly until wriggled out of my arms, begging me to stop. To them, their mum must have just seemed extra soppy today. But for me, I wanted to make sure they knew I loved them just in case something bad happened tonight.

With that done, I made my way home, feeling sick with anxiety the whole way there as I thought about what William might be plotting. He'll know I don't trust him now, so he'll have to do something about that. But I know that whatever he is going to do, just like whatever he has done in the past, is going to be very hard to prove unless I have some real, irrefutable evidence. Without Adelina and David around, and with Becky seemingly too worried to talk to me openly, I have to find a way of coaxing the truth from William myself.

But I'll only get that if he believes there is no real threat posed by him telling me.

So, what's his plan? It's too much of a coincidence for him to suggest we have a quiet night in together on the day he was looking at my phone. So he's planning something for tonight, and when he texts to say the takeaway has been ordered and he's on his way home, I know I don't have long left to figure it out.

It's a little after seven o'clock when I hear William's key turning in the lock, and I put down my glass of wine as he enters the kitchen with a big smile on his face.

'Ahh, you've opened a bottle already,' he says, and he grabs a glass from the cupboard before pouring himself a hearty measure.

I watch him as he holds his glass out towards me, wanting me to toast with him.

'Cheers. Here's to a lovely evening,' he says as our glasses clink together. 'Just the two of us.'

'Cheers,' I reply, determined to pretend everything is normal, just as he seems to be.

'The food should be here soon,' he tells me. 'I don't know about you, but I'm starving.'

'Yeah, I'm hungry.'

'I ordered us extra poppadoms and a few more sauces. I hope you don't mind.'

'Of course not.'

'Good. I'm sure we'll eat it all.'

I see him check his watch then before he takes another drink. He looks a little nervous. On edge. Like he can't quite settle. If I didn't know better, I would put it down to him needing a little bit of time – and maybe another glass of wine – to unwind after work. But I do know better, don't I? I know that everything this man does is not always what it seems.

If only I had stopped things there before they went any further. But I let things play out. I allowed William to do his thing.

By the time the doorbell rang to let us both know that the delivery driver was here, there was no going back.

36

WILLIAM

After I've received the bag full of food from the polite delivery driver at our door, I suggest to Maria that she light a candle and put on some music while I serve the food up. She did that, and by the time I have our meals on our plates, the atmosphere is rather pleasant in our dining room.

It's almost a shame that it will soon be ruined.

There surely can't be many things that could spoil a 'romantic' dinner quite as much as one of the diners suffering a severe allergic reaction halfway through. But that's exactly what is about to happen here as I eagerly wait for Maria to tuck into the curry I ordered for her, a curry that she's had many times before and is one that she usually enjoys greatly. But she isn't going to like it tonight, and as much as it is going to hurt me to see her suffer once the peanuts take effect, I consider it a necessary evil to keep the sins of my past buried.

Maria starts with a poppadom, as do I, and as we crunch away on them, she asks me if I would ever consider selling the business and retiring early.

'Not for a long time yet,' I reply. 'Why? Would you?'

'I don't know. I have been having some thoughts about it lately. Wondering if there might be more to life than just working so hard.'

'Like what?'

'I don't know. I was just thinking about some of the people who have left our company and wondering what they might be doing now. Whether or not they're happier for making a change. People like Becky.'

'Becky? Why her?'

'I saw her the other day. We bumped into each other.'

'Oh, that's nice.'

I know my wife is toying with me now, but she can play games all she wants because she's running on borrowed time. She just doesn't know it yet.

'Yeah, she said she's very happy in her new job. Didn't seem like she had many regrets. Well, apart from one thing.'

'And what was that?'

I carefully spoon some mango chutney onto my poppadom.

'She told me she was unsure if she handled the whole David situation as well as she might have.'

'Really? I thought she handled it very well.'

'That didn't seem to be how she saw it. She seemed to think he might have been innocent.'

I munch my way through the rest of the poppadom, holding my wife's gaze before I ask, 'You didn't tell her about him threatening us, did you?'

'No, of course not. But it was interesting to hear her thoughts. And it has made me feel a little bit better about what happened with David. You know, how you gave him the money. Maybe he deserved it.'

'Oh good. Shall we start our mains?' I suggest, trying not to snap, as I'm growing impatient now. I want to speed this whole thing up. But Maria takes her time and continues to nibble at her starter.

'I met somebody else as well,' Maria goes on. 'A friend of Adelina's.'

'You have been busy,' I say, keeping my face neutral. 'And what were you doing meeting her?'

'I've been trying to track Adelina down. I wanted to make sure she was okay.'

'And how did that go? Did you find her?'

'Nope. It's as if she vanished into thin air.'

'Unlikely. I'm sure she's happily at home in Albania. Mmmm, this is delicious,' I say, eating my own curry. 'You should eat yours before it goes cold.'

'It's okay for another minute. Anyway, like I said, I met a friend of Adelina's, but while she had no idea what might have happened to her, she did tell me something interesting.'

'And what was that?'

'She told me that Adelina mentioned a few times that her boss could be a bit of a flirt.'

My curry suddenly isn't quite so tasty. I stop eating as Maria stares at me.

'I think she was talking about you,' she confirms. 'So is it true? Did you flirt with Adelina?'

'Well, no, not really. I mean, I was friendly but no different than with anybody else.'

'So you didn't find her attractive?'

'No.'

'You didn't try anything with her?'

'No.'

'Are you sure? You see, I'm thinking you were perhaps the one who sexually harassed her.'

Yep, she's got me. She's figured it out. At least, she's sussed how this whole thing started anyway. But she hasn't eaten her damn curry and choked to death yet, so I can't quite admit it for now.

'Maria! What the hell kind of accusation is that? Of course I didn't harass her!'

She stares at me for a very awkward, quiet moment, and the fact that the song playing in the background ends and the new one doesn't start for a few seconds only adds to the unsettling silence.

'Don't worry, William. Whatever happened between you two, I know you sorted it out,' Maria replies.

That wasn't quite what I expected her to say. 'What do you mean?'

'I'm just saying that I'm sure you did whatever you needed to do. To protect the company. Yourself. *Us.*'

Is she saying she knows I've done something wrong but doesn't care about it?

If so, maybe I don't have to kill her after all.

Maria picks up her fork and prepares to tuck into her curry.

'Wait!' I say, holding out my hand across the table to get her to slow down.

'What's wrong?'

'What did you mean about me doing whatever I needed to do to protect us?' I ask, and Maria shrugs.

'I meant exactly that. I'm sure that whatever happened, you did what was best for us. Like you always do, right?'

Maria has some of her curry on her fork now, and once it goes in her mouth, it will be too late. If I'm going to save her, I need to do it now.

'It's time for the truth,' I say, and that gives her reason to pause.

'What do you mean?'

'I want the truth. What exactly do you think I've done?'

'Excuse me?'

'Stop playing games. Just ask me whatever it is you want to ask me.'

Maria puts her fork back down then, and I wait to see what her question will be.

'Did you do something to Adelina?' she asks.

'Be more specific.'

'Did you kill her?'

I hold eye contact with my wife for several seconds before shaking my head.

'No, of course not.'

I couldn't do it. I couldn't admit it to her, at least not while she is still in a healthy state. But her question has confirmed that she is on the right track in terms of figuring out what I've done.

'And David?'

Wow, she's gone there too. She's bold, I'll give her that.

'No,' I reply firmly. 'Is that what you think? That I'm a murderer?'

'I don't know what to think anymore. You've been lying to me, a lot, so of course I'm wondering what else you could be hiding.'

As I sit there and look at my wife, who is potentially so close to death but doesn't know it yet, I realise that all of this is down to me. Every lie I ever told and every mistake I ever made is now the reason Maria's life has to end. But, just like with Adelina and David, I'll do whatever I need to do to stay out of trouble. I'll never be able to fully relax with Maria suspecting me, which means she has to go.

She has to eat.

I pick my fork up then and resume eating my curry, and I watch as Maria picks her fork up too. And then it begins. She starts eating, starts consuming the sauce that includes peanuts, meaning a clock has already started ticking towards death inside her body.

I know her allergic reactions to be severe, but I also know that they take a few moments to come on. The last time she suffered such a reaction was when we had gone out for dinner with friends during a weekend trip to London. In hindsight, going for a meal at an unfamiliar Thai restaurant was risky, and despite Maria informing the staff of her allergy, her food was still tainted and she had begun struggling to breathe not long after tucking into her meal. Fortunately, she had her EpiPen in her handbag, and I had used it, saving the day and possibly saving the restaurant owner from going to prison for manslaughter.

But there will be no use of the EpiPen tonight.

With time running out for my wife now, I can finally relax and admit all the things that I've been hiding. No consequences can come from confessing to a dead person.

'You shouldn't have doubted me,' I tell Maria as she keeps eating. 'You should have just taken my word for things and carried on. If only you had, then everything would have been okay.'

'What do you mean?' Maria asks me, her mouthful of chicken korma and rice.

'I know you've been snooping around behind my back. I know you've been looking at private investigators. And I know you've been thinking about going to the police.'

Maria stops chewing then, but the damage will already be done, so she can do whatever she likes now, while she still has time.

'You should have carried on being the good wife,' I tell her. 'Do your work. Raise the kids. Leave me to figure out what's best for the family. But no, you decided to stop trusting me, and that's why I've had to do what I've done.'

'Which is what? What have you done?'

'I'm sorry.'

'William, what have you done?'

My eyes drift down to Maria's plate, and she stares at her food before I notice it begin. She puts a hand to her throat. She clears it. She looks nervous.

And then she tells me she thinks she is having an allergic reaction.

'Peanuts!' she cries. 'I need my EpiPen now! William, you have to help me.'

She goes to get up from her seat, but I tell her that I'll get it, and she is to stay calm and drink some water. As I leave the room, I am in no hurry and simply loiter in the hallway outside the dining room before returning to see how Maria is getting on. Not well by the looks of things. She's on the floor now, curled up on the carpet, gasping for air and clutching her throat, her eyes wide and full of fear as she looks up at me and begs me to help her.

But I don't. I just pull my chair up beside where she lies and take a seat before brushing a few poppadum crumbs off my shirt and letting out a deep sigh.

'You should be grateful. I strangled Adelina with my bare hands, and I stamped on David's head with my feet. This isn't quite so brutal, right?'

Maria can't answer me as she continues to make awful gargling noises on the floor below me.

'Yes, I killed them both. But I had no choice. They threat-ened everything we had worked so hard to build. Our company. Our family. I couldn't lose all that over one silly mistake. If only Adelina had reacted differently when I tried to kiss her, she'd be alive now, as would David. And as would you.'

Maria is falling quieter now, her body still twitching, but the fight for life leaving her by the minute.

'I'll look after our children. I promise you that. And I'll make sure our company continues to flourish. You don't have to worry about any of it. Just relax now. Close your eyes. Let go.'

I watch the breath ebb out of my wife before she falls still. Then I say goodbye to her before taking a sip from my glass of wine because it's the last time I'll be able to savour something so nice for a while. In a moment, I'm going to have to call 999 and ask for an ambulance. When the paramedics arrive, I'll have to stand by and play the part of the distressed husband. Then, after they've told me that my wife is dead, I'll have to let the children know, as well as Maria's parents. I'll also have to speak to the police, because they're sure to have a few questions, but I'll answer them all with one very sorry and very heartfelt apology. I'll apologise because I'll tell them that when I ordered our usual Indian takeaway tonight that, in the process, I completely forgot to mention that my wife has a peanut allergy.

They'll understand. They'll know this wasn't my fault. They'll be devastated for me, but, most importantly, they won't be interested in prosecuting me because it will look like this was all a terrible, tragic accident.

Then, and only then, once all of that is done, will I be able to relax.

'Okay, let's get this over with,' I say as I take out my phone and call the emergency services.

The call is answered quickly, and my demeanour changes just as fast as I switch from the cold, calculated man I was a moment ago into the panicked, distraught husband I now need to be.

After I've told the operator what has happened and where we are, she tells me that help is on its way before instructing me to stay on the line because she can give me advice as to how to perform CPR on my ailing wife. I pretend to listen to what she is saying and also to carry out her instructions but, in reality, I'm sitting casually in my chair, staring down at Maria's corpse and thinking about how I won't have to sneak around when I sleep with other women now.

'It's not working!' I cry down the phone as I make believe that the CPR isn't doing the job, and then I hear the knock at the door that tells me the paramedics have arrived.

I run to let them in, telling them to hurry and to do what they can because I can't lose my wife, I just can't. I'm not crying yet, but I'm damn well trying my best to summon up a few tears as I lead the paramedics into the dining room and watch as they kneel down beside Maria and check her vitals.

I'm ready for them to tell me that she's gone. I'm ready for the next part of this whole charade to begin. Most of all, I'm ready for all of this to be over.

But what happens next is something that I was definitely not ready for.

The paramedics share a confused glance as Maria opens her eyes and smiles at them.

Then she sits up, as right as rain.

I feel like all the air is being sucked out of the room as she smiles at me too.

Then she points to something in the corner. Something over on the bookshelf, propped up beside the Best Business Award we won not so long ago.

Something that looks very much like a phone.

And the camera is facing the table.

EPILOGUE

MARIA

In hindsight, William must regret making all those bad jokes for so many years. They're the ones in which he jested that he always knew the best way to kill me off if he ever needed to, thanks to my allergic reaction to peanuts and all. Of course, at the time, nobody who was privy to such a witticism would have ever thought that William was serious, least of all me, and I'm sure he never actually meant it either. But things change, and in our case, they changed very fast.

I figured out what my husband was up to when he suggested the Indian takeaway and told me he would order it. As has been the case throughout our entire relationship when ordering any food that I might consume, one thing always has to happen. And that is that we strictly request that the meal contains no nuts. Sometimes it's me who makes that request, and sometimes it's William, but all that matters is that one of us tells whoever is preparing the food that there would be serious repercussions if it contained my allergen. That's why I decided to phone the restaurant in question and specifically ask them if my husband had stated my allergy when giving the order.

They told me he hadn't, and that's when I knew what he was going to do to me.

Of course it hurt to know that my husband was definitely going to try to kill me, but I didn't have much time to wallow in self-pity. So what I did was simply tell the man at the restaurant to alter the order so that no nuts would be present. He said that wouldn't be a problem, and I thanked him before asking him if he would be so kind as to not mention my phone call to my husband when the delivery driver dropped the food off, because I didn't want him to feel bad about making a mistake that could have such dire consequences for me. The waiter assured me that no one would mention it, and with that our little secret, I ended the call and got myself ready to give the acting performance of my life.

While setting the dining table for our upcoming meal, I did something that didn't usually feature in my pre-dinner routine. I positioned my phone on the bookshelf near the table so that the camera was facing where my husband and I would be eating, and then I set the camera to start recording. I wanted to make sure I captured everything that happened, most of all the part where William would presumably react very nonchalantly to the fact that his wife was dying right in front of his eyes.

I had no idea that he would confess to the murders of Adelina and David. I'd thought the fact that he'd tried to kill me would have been enough to land him in serious trouble, but he really buried himself by admitting to all the terrible things he had done. The footage of him watching me 'die' has been enough to convince the police that he believed peanuts were in my meal and that the 'reaction' I was suffering was a very real one. In reality, my anaphylactic shock was pure charade, because there was nothing in my food that could cause me any problem. All I had to do was match William's expectations and pretend like there was.

I only stopped acting once the paramedics arrived because I knew it would be impossible to fool them. But I didn't need to fool them. I only needed to fool William, and that's exactly what I did.

After realising I had tricked him, William tried to talk his way out of it, just as he usually does. But after I handed my phone with the incriminating video on it to the paramedics, asking them to contact the police, my husband tried to make a quick getaway. But he hadn't got very far because his precious car was blocked in by the ambulance at the top of the driveway. He pleaded with the paramedics to move it, but they unsurprisingly decided they would rather wait until the police turned up.

It was a sobering sight to watch my husband being taken into custody after I confirmed that he had tried to kill me, and not just because the handcuffs around his wrists reminded me of the night David had restrained us in hand-cuffs of his own. But, however shaken and overcome by adrenaline I felt, I was also hugely relieved to have emerged from the whole situation unscathed. And, of course, it was a tremendous relief to see my children and parents again, although I found it far from easy to explain to them exactly what had happened.

While I gave my parents all the details of the harrowing truth about their son-in-law, I kept much of what their dad was guilty of back from Edward and Penny. I didn't mention the murders, or the fact that he had attempted to kill me, deciding instead to simply tell them that he had made some mistakes and would have to go and live in a place where people are punished for such things. I'm not totally naïve, though, and I realise that one day very soon they will almost certainly find out exactly what their dad did, but I'll deal with that problem in the future. For now, we're safe, and I can hold them in my arms again. That's all that matters.

Despite the evidence against him, William chose to plead 'not guilty' to the crimes he was accused of, meaning a trial was necessary to determine his guilt and punishment. I attended every moment of that trial, not because I wanted to see him suffer but because I wanted to know if my husband had kept any other secrets from me. It turned out that there were, the biggest of which was that he had bought himself a second property across town and had stayed there on numerous occasions while pretending to me that he was working late. The court heard from one of his neighbours at this second home, a dour man called Ken, and he spoke of the night he caught William in handcuffs. Even in Ken's monotone, it sounded like a truly bizarre encounter, made all the stranger by the fact that I was – unbeknownst to Ken – imprisoned in the trunk of the car and also by the horrible truth that William had only just killed David inside the house.

Naturally, I was in court to see the verdict delivered, as were members of Adelina's and David's families. We watched as William was found guilty on all counts of murder and attempted murder and sentenced to life imprisonment for his crimes. A few people in the public gallery wept when the sentence was handed down, but I stayed strong, not wishing to be seen as weak when I knew my husband would more than likely steal a glance at me just before he was taken away. And sure enough, he did look in my direction, and when he did, he mouthed something to me.

Two words.

'I'm sorry.'

But, sadly, it was far too late for apologies, and while he has since repeatedly requested for me and the children to visit him behind bars, we have refused to do so. I doubt we ever will.

It's not easy to move on after all I've been through, but I was determined to do so for the sake of myself and my children. My first problem was what to do with the business that I owned with my husband. Despite the stories of his shocking crimes making headline news across the country, business hadn't been affected too badly. To my genuine surprise, our clients seemed to understand that our association with a double murderer didn't make the rest of us criminals too – and they continued to be willing to work with us. Perhaps the scandal actually attracted new business too, which struck me as almost comically ironic given that so much of what William did was motivated by his desperation to prevent Gallagher's reputation from being tarnished.

Even so, after thinking long and hard about it, I decided that I was going to sell the business. Potential buyers weren't too hard to come by; after all, the company William and I founded together had a proven track record of being profitable and scalable. After agreeing on a considerable price and ensuring that all current employees would retain their jobs if they so chose, I officially severed all ties with the business and focused on the next part of my life.

This was mainly going to consist of being a full-time mum to two children who were unlucky enough to have a despicable father. But I made sure to allocate some of the proceeds from the sale to two other families who I felt deserved a little support. I gave six-figure sums to the families of both Adelina and David, and while I knew money could never replace what my husband took from them, I hoped it would go some way to easing their pain and showing them that not everybody in this world is bad.

Looking ahead, I have lots I want to do, not least of which is to take Edward and Penny on a trip to Disney World. It'll do us good to get out of our town for a while, away from the journalists, who camped out on our doorstep for far too long, and the members of the public who stop and stare at us every time we go shopping in the supermarket. Who knows? Maybe we won't come back. Maybe we'll start a new life overseas. The future feels a little scary because it's so uncertain. But I'm determined to stay positive; I tell myself that I've been through plenty of other scary times and survived.

To think all this started, for me at least, with David breaking into our home and threatening me with a knife. If only I had locked my front door, he might still be alive. Nothing could have saved Adelina, but I might not have found out my husband had been lying to me, and so he might never have ended up going to prison. Or maybe it all would have played out like it did in the end, regardless. Fate. Destiny. Bad luck. *All of the above.*

Given the webs of deceit and violence he'd already woven around himself, our business and our family, any or all of these could have caught up with my husband.

Do I wish that front door had been shut and potentially altered my future?

Do I wish I was still living in blissful ignorance?

It would be easy to say no, because we like to think that the truth should always come out, but I don't know. It's not that simple. My life was good before.

Now it's different.

I have David to thank and blame for that.

ABOUT THE AUTHOR

Did you enjoy *The Intruder*? Please consider leaving a review on Amazon to help other readers discover the book.

Daniel Hurst writes psychological thrillers and loves to tell tales about unusual things happening to normal people. He has written all his life, making the progression from handing scribbled stories to his parents as a boy to writing full length novels in his thirties. He lives in the North West of England and when he isn't writing, he is usually watching a game of football in a pub where his wife can't find him.

Want to connect with Daniel? Visit him at his website or on any of these social media channels.

www.danielhurstbooks.com

ALSO BY DANIEL HURST

INKUBATOR TITLES

THE BOYFRIEND

(A Psychological Thriller)

THE PASSENGER

(A Psychological Thriller)

THE PROMOTION

(A Psychological Thriller)

THE NEW FRIENDS

(A Psychological Thriller)

THE BREAK

(A Psychological Thriller)

THE ACCIDENT

(A Psychological Thriller)

THE INTRUDER

(A Psychological Thriller)

Made in the USA
Columbia, SC
06 May 2023

7cdfdeb1-fa7c-4e97-9d34-353e7096559fR01